Visit with characters introduced in the acclaimed
Desire Trilogy by Joan Hohl!

"Miss Vanzant?"

he said in a deep, surprisingly beautiful voice. The
sun was at his back, leaving his face in shadow. All
Nicole could see was that he was tall and rangy, and
he held a wide-brimmed hat in his left hand.

"Yes." Nicole swallowed to ease the dryness in
her throat.

"I'm Josh Barnet, Thack's foreman," he said,
slowly walking toward her. "My orders were to
watch out for you in case you got lost." Amusement
enhanced the richness of his voice. "Are you lost?"

Nicole managed a breathless laugh. "I'm not sure."
As he drew to within a few feet of her, Nicole's
breath constricted in her chest, and she felt a wave of
shock cascade down her spine.

Up close the man looked intimidating. Josh Barnet
was not exactly slender but whip-cord lean. His
skin was dark, and it stretched tautly over high
cheekbones. His thin lips possessed not a hint of
sensual fullness. Collectively his features gave the
impression that here was one formidable character!
Nicole had to fight a sudden urge to turn and run—
all the way back to Pennsylvania.

Dear Reader:

Series and Spin-offs! Connecting characters and intriguing interconnections to make your head whirl.

In Joan Hohl's successful trilogy for Silhouette Desire—*Texas Gold* (7/86), *California Copper* (10/86), *Nevada Silver* (1/87)—Joan created a cast of characters that just wouldn't quit. You figure out how *Lady Ice* (5/87) connects. And in August, "J.B." demanded his own story—*One Tough Hombre*. In *Falcon's Flight*, coming in November, you'll learn *all* about . . .?

Annette Broadrick's *Return to Yesterday* (6/87) introduced Adam St. Clair. This August *Adam's Story* tells about the woman who saves his life—and teaches him a thing or two about love!

The six Branigan brothers appeared in Leslie Davis Guccione's *Bittersweet Harvest* (10/86) and *Still Waters* (5/87). September brings *Something in Common*, where the eldest of the strapping Irishmen finds love in unexpected places.

Midnight Rambler by Linda Barlow is in October—a special Halloween surprise, and totally unconnected to anything.

Keep an eye out for other Silhouette Desire favorites—Diana Palmer, Dixie Browning, Ann Major and Elizabeth Lowell, to name a few. You never know when secondary characters will insist on their own story. . . .

All the best,

Isabel Swift
Senior Editor & Editorial Coordinator
Silhouette Books

JOAN HOHL
One Tough Hombre

Silhouette Desire

Published by Silhouette Books New York

America's Publisher of Contemporary Romance

SILHOUETTE BOOKS
300 East 42nd St., New York, N.Y. 10017

Copyright © 1987 by Joan Hohl

ISBN: 0-373-05372-X

First Silhouette Books printing August 1987

America's Publisher of Contemporary Romance

Printed in the U.S.A.

Books by Joan Hohl

Silhouette Special Edition

Thorne's Way #54

Silhouette Intimate Moments

Moments Harsh, Moments Gentle #35

Silhouette Romance

A Taste for Rich Things #334
Someone Waiting #358
The Scent of Lilacs #376

Silhouette Desire

A Much Needed Holiday #247
* *Texas Gold* #294
* *California Copper* #312
* *Nevada Silver* #330
Lady Ice #354
One Tough Hombre #372

* Desire Trilogy

JOAN HOHL,

a Gemini and an inveterate daydreamer, says she always has her head in the clouds. Though she reads eight or nine books a week, she only discovered romances ten years ago. "But as soon as I read one," she confesses, "I was hooked." Now an extremely popular author, she is thrilled to be getting paid for exactly what she loves doing best. Joan Hohl also writes under the pseudonym Amii Lorin.

For my editor, Tara Hughes—because she loved the Hombre from the very beginning!

One

"Nicole, you look fantastic!"

Her laughter at odds with the tears sparkling in her eyes, Nicole Vanzant ran into the welcoming arms of a friend she had not seen for almost four years.

"Oh, Barbara, it's so good to see you!" Nicole hugged her friend fiercely, then moved back to sweep an all-encompassing glance over her, from her gleaming red-brown hair to her slender feet encased in leather sandals. "And talk about looking good!" Nicole's dark eyebrows arched appreciatively. "If this is what married life does to a woman, maybe I'd better try it." Nicole's gaze settled on Barbara's happy face. "I've never seen you looking lovelier."

"Even with the ten pounds I've acquired?" Barbara asked with a grin.

"The ten pounds look great on you."

"Are you two planning on standing in the yard all afternoon just smiling at each other?"

Both women swung around, Barbara's grin softening, Nicole's eyes widening at the sight of the man leaning indolently against a wrought-iron porch support that gave a Spanish flavor to the large two-story house. The man's appearance was enough to widen any woman's eyes, regardless of her age. He was very tall and slender, with burnished skin and white-gold hair. And he was, without doubt, one of the most handsome men Nicole had ever seen.

Was this gorgeous hunk of cowboy Barbara's husband? Nicole wondered, turning her questioning gaze back to her friend.

"Come meet the big bad Texan." Barbara's eyes danced with anticipation. Looping a tanned arm around Nicole's waist, she began walking toward the house—and the smiling man waiting for them.

As they approached the three stone steps up to the porch, he moved back to pull the screen door open. "It's one whole helluva lot cooler in the house," he drawled, motioning the women in.

"Thack!" Barbara protested his language as she ushered Nicole into the foyer.

"Barb, honey, I'm sure Nicole has heard the word *hell* before," Thack said as he trailed inside after them.

The interior of the house felt deliciously cool. Sighing with relief at escaping the relentless Texas sun, Nicole glanced quickly around the surprisingly elegant foyer as she turned to meet her host.

"Nicole, my husband, Thackery Sharp." Pride and the closest thing to adoration that Nicole had ever seen glowed from Barbara's eyes. "Thack," she continued, "this is my friend—"

"Nicole Vanzant," Thack finished for his wife in a low, contemplative tone. Grasping her hand, he held it for a long moment while studying her with a narrowed gaze.

Nicole grew uneasy under his scrutiny and had to fight the urge to cover her cheek with her free hand. The scar she'd been left with as a result of a car accident was faint, but it was there. Nicole never forgot it was there. She was beginning to feel uncomfortable when Thack released her hand.

"God, honey," he said, slicing a look at Barbara. "You were right on the money when you described Nicole to me." His brown eyes shifted back to Nicole's face. "I'm sorry," he said, "I didn't mean to be rude by speaking to Barb as if you weren't here." His incredible white-blond hair shimmered as he shook his head. "I felt poleaxed. Lady, you are one beautiful woman, and that's a fact. But what Barbara didn't mention was that you have the most compassionate eyes." He paused, as if searching for words, then added simply, "If I felt in need of understanding, I wouldn't hesitate to come to you."

Uncertain how to respond to such a statement, Nicole stared at him mutely for a second, then, with bubbling laughter, she hugged him every bit as fiercely as she had his wife.

"Thank you, Thackery," she murmured. "Even though I know it's not true, hearing it does wonders for my ego."

"Nicole!" Barbara cried.

"Wait a minute." Thack's firm voice overrode Barbara's. "Let's get two things straight before we go any further here." One blond eyebrow arched imperiously. "First," he said sternly, "I was stating a fact, not buttering up your ego. Got that?" When Nicole nodded, a smile eased his features. "Secondly," he went on in a teasing drawl, "I'm Thack to my friends, whose ranks I hope you'll soon be joining."

"Where do I enlist?" Nicole asked seriously.

"You enlist after you've met the rest of the family and settled in," Barbara inserted, taking her hand to lead her up the wide central staircase and along a hallway to the right wing of the house. "You must feel tired, sticky and hungry." Tilting her head, she raised her brows quizzically.

"A little tired, very sticky and marginally hungry," Nicole laughed, frowning inwardly at Barbara's use of the word *family*. Barbara had invited her to spend the entire summer at the ranch, but if Thack had relatives visiting, Nicole didn't want to intrude. "The flight was tiring, but I got a few hours' sleep at a motel outside Houston early this morning."

Barbara paused at a closed door halfway down the carpeted hallway. "You should have called to tell us your flight number. Someone would have met you at the plane. There was no reason to rent a car and drive out here." As she finished scolding, Barbara gently turned the knob and pushed the door open, motioning for Nicole to precede her into the room.

"Well, I decided to come earlier than expected, and there was a seat available on the red-eye flight, so..." Nicole's voice faded as she entered the room she'd thought was the guest room. The walls were painted white and pink. Frilly pink dotted-swiss curtains prevented some of the harsh afternoon sunlight from streaming in the one wide window. A soft carpet of a deep rose color cushioned her footsteps. Nicole saw and appreciated the decor but what caught her attention was the white canopied crib placed along a side wall. Her breath catching in her throat, Nicole walked slowly to the crib, her eyes stinging from a rush of tears as she gazed at the sleeping baby curled up in it.

"Oh, Barbara!" Nicole's gasp was muted by wonder. "She's beautiful." Tentatively she reached over the high side of the crib to stroke the tiny satiny cheek.

"Yes. I can hardly believe she's mine."

"And mine," Thack said, coming into the room to stand beside his wife.

A tiny smile curved Nicole's lips as she detected the emotion woven in Thack's tone. Male pride and possession were there along with blatant love. But overriding all else was a note of incredible wonder.

"Congratulations," she murmured, caressing the child with a soft gaze. "She's beautiful, and so tiny!" Sheer wonder coated Nicole's tone and brightened her eyes. "When was she born?"

Barbara and Thack smiled at Nicole, then at each other. "She arrived two weeks ago yesterday," Barbara answered. "Three weeks ahead of schedule," she added with a grin.

"What's her name?" Nicole asked.

"Rita." The proud parents answered as one.

"After my grandmother," Thack continued. "She was beautiful, too. She died when I was ten."

"I'm sorry." Nicole murmured the words automatically. "I'm sure she would have felt honored to have your daughter named for her." Nicole reluctantly drew her gaze away from the baby's silky blond curls. "May I hold her after she wakes up?" she asked as she turned to face them.

"Well, of course you can!" Barbara exclaimed softly, grasping Nicole's hand. "But right now let's get you settled in. Aunt Ellie has a snack ready for you, and she's waiting to meet you."

Aunt Ellie? Nicole thought with chagrin. Obviously Barbara and Thack did have at least one relative visiting, probably to help with the new baby. She really should have confirmed her arrival before rushing away from Philadelphia, but Barbara had been so enthused when Nicole had agreed to visit that Nicole had come on the spur of the moment. Her spirits drooping, Nicole trailed her host and hostess from the nursery and along the hallway to a room near the back of the sprawling ranch house. As Barbara reached for the doorknob, a call echoed the length of the long hallway.

"The bags are in the foyer, Thackery."

"Dammit!" the tall rancher muttered, swinging around to lope back down the passageway.

Nicole watched him depart, a frown tugging her eyebrows together. "What—" she began, only to be cut off by Barbara's soft laughter.

"Don't mind Thack," she advised, ushering Nicole into the room. "He gets impatient with Aunt Ellie."

Oh, great. Nicole groaned silently, her shoulders slumping as she stepped into the guest room. Not only had her unannounced arrival been an intrusion, but she had also stumbled into a tense family situation.

"The room's lovely," Nicole complimented sincerely, appreciating the warm ambiance of the cherrywood furniture in the burgundy-and-white setting. "But I really don't think I should stay."

"Not stay!" Barbara said with a gasp.

"What are you talking about?" Thack demanded, striding into the room with Nicole's suitcase and flight bag. "You just got here." Heaving the bags onto the bed, he pivoted to face her, his hands on his slim hips.

If Thack's intention had been intimidation, he succeeded admirably. Nicole stepped back. "I...I should have let you know I was coming," she explained haltingly. "You already have company, and..." Her voice faded as Thack grinned.

"That's not company," he drawled. "That's Aunt Ellie." Still grinning, he ambled to the door. "Welcome to the Sharp spread, Nicole. I'll see you later." Thack winked at his wife, then strode from the room.

"Now what is this nonsense about leaving?" Barbara asked, mirroring her husband's actions by placing her much smaller hands on her gently rounded hips.

Nicole shrugged. "Well, I thought since you already had a visitor, in addition to a new infant, you probably didn't need an old friend cluttering up the place."

Deciding her friend was still running away from life, Barbara felt a tug at her heart, much the same as she felt every time she looked at her precious baby. Nicole at times seemed like a lost child. Barbara's recently activated maternal instincts clamored for her to reassure Nicole. Smiling gently, she grasped Nicole's hand and led her to the settee by the window.

"As Thack said, Nicole, you *are* welcome here." Seating herself next to Nicole, Barbara clasped her other hand. "And we didn't need notice of your arrival."

"But you have company," Nicole insisted.

Barbara shook her head. "No, we don't. Thack was telling the truth. My Aunt Ellie isn't company. She lives here with us. She is part of the family."

Relief shivered through Nicole. She didn't want to leave. Strangely, though she hadn't seen Barbara for over three years, she felt more at home with her than she had with anyone else, including her brother, whom she adored.

"Oh, Barbara, it is good to see you again," Nicole whispered, emotion tightening her throat.

"And it's wonderful to see you again." Barbara ran an assaying gaze over Nicole's slim form. "What little there is of you," she said, shaking her head. "And there'll be no more talk about leaving?" she asked in a tone as tight as Nicole's had been.

"No," Nicole said decisively.

"Good." Barbara nodded briskly, squeezing Nicole's hands. Then she stood. "Now I'll leave you to freshen up. Take your time," she went on, moving to the door. "But remember, there's food and coffee waiting for you in the kitchen."

"Okay." Nicole glanced around, then indicated a door to her left. "The bathroom?" she asked hopefully.

"Yes," Barbara replied, laughing.

"And how do I find the kitchen?"

"Backtrack along the hallway to the foyer," Barbara instructed, "then turn right and follow your nose."

Laughing to herself, Nicole walked to the bed to dig her makeup case from the flight bag. As she crossed to the bathroom her lips curved into a smile. It was good to be with friends, she mused.

As she applied a light covering of fresh makeup, Nicole took extra care with the faint white scar that ran from her cheekbone near her right temple to a point midway along her jawline. When she had finished, she scrutinized her reflection in the mirror, her eyes narrowed. So intent was her gaze on the scar that Nicole didn't take note of the flawless beauty of the rest of her face. Then, as if bored with her image, she sighed and turned from the mirror and left the bathroom.

Following instructions, Nicole retraced their earlier path to the foyer. Standing irresolute, she glanced around. To the left ran another more narrow passageway with closed doors to several rooms. To her right was a double doorway, the doors open to reveal a spacious living room. Beyond the living room Nicole could see a large dining room. Was the kitchen off the dining room? she wondered. Deciding to find out, she strolled into the living room, then stopped abruptly, a gasped *"Oh!"* bursting from her lips as her gaze collided with a man standing at the sliding glass doors that took up most of the wall opposite the entranceway. At her startled sound he turned to face her. The sun was at his back, leaving his face in shadow. All Nicole could see was that he was tall and rangy, and he held a wide-brimmed hat in his left hand.

"Miss Vanzant?" he said in a deep, surprisingly beautiful voice.

"Yes." Nicole swallowed to ease the dryness in her throat caused by his unexpected appearance.

"I'm Josh Barnet, Thack's foreman," he said, slowly walking toward her. "My orders were to watch out for you, in case you got lost." Amusement enhanced the richness of his voice. "Are you lost, Miss Vanzant?"

Nicole managed a breathless laugh. "I'm not sure," she admitted candidly. "I was just about to search out the kitchen by way of the dining room." As he drew to within a few feet of her, Nicole's breath constricted in her chest, and she felt a wave of shock cascade down her spine.

Up close the man looked intimidating. Josh Barnet was not exactly slender but, more accurately, whipcord lean. His skin was dark in contrast to Thack's golden burnish, and it stretched tautly over high cheekbones, a straight nose and a jawline that seemed almost hewn from granite. There were hollows under his eyes and in his cheeks. His thin lips possessed not a hint of sensual fullness. Collectively, his features gave the impression that here was one formidable character! Nicole had to fight a sudden urge to turn and run—all the way back to the safety of her home in Pennsylvania.

"You would have found what you were searching for."

Bemused by the disquieting thoughts he aroused in her, Nicole gazed at him uncomprehendingly. "What?" she asked blankly.

"The kitchen." Josh Barnet's thin lips twitched with an inner amusement. "You were heading in the right direction." A ghost of a smile played over his mouth as he flicked the hat he held at his side. "Forge ahead," he advised. "I'll bring up the rear."

What an odd man, Nicole thought, sweeping by him regally. *I wonder what cave Thack found him in.*

And it's a damned fetching rear at that. Silent laughter tickled Josh Barnet's throat. Ambling behind Nicole Vanzant, he sent his curious gaze over the rest of her body, whistling soundlessly as his glance slowly glided the length of her long, slender legs to her delicate ankles. *The rest of her ain't exactly dog meat, either,* he concluded just as she entered the kitchen.

"Oh, Nicole, your timing's perfect!" Barbara greeted her as she arrived in the kitchen. "Aunt Ellie just made a fresh pot of coffee." She held out her hand. "Come over here and meet my aunt."

A tentative smile curving her lips, Nicole walked over to the tall, gaunt woman. Pondering if all Texans had a forbidding look about them at first, she slowly extended her hand as Barbara made the introductions.

"Nicole, my aunt, Ellie Holcomb." Barbara smiled. "Aunt Ellie, this is Nicole Vanzant."

The older woman's grip was brief but strong. For an instant Nicole felt speared by Ellie's sharp gaze. Then the woman smiled, relieving the stern lines marking her weathered face.

"You're a right pretty young woman, Nicole," Ellie said warmly. "And it's a pleasure to finally meet you."

"Thank you," Nicole responded on a pleased, breathy laugh. "It's a pleasure to meet you, too."

"And you've already met J.B.," Barbara said.

"J.B.?" Nicole frowned.

"I introduced myself as Josh."

Nicole turned at the sound of his beautiful voice and felt her breath constricting as it had moments before in the living room. The bright sunlight pouring into the room intensified the spare harshness of his features. But it was only one of those features that had caused her chest contraction this time. Josh Barnet had breathtakingly beautiful sapphire blue eyes. Captivated by their brilliance, Nicole stared numbly at him.

"If you'll let me call you Nicki, I'll let you call me J.B.," he said.

Nicki? Nicole frowned. No one had ever called her Nicki, not even Peter. Surprisingly, Nicole discovered that she rather liked the sound of the nickname.

"Nicki! I love it!" Barbara exclaimed.

"So do I." Thack backed up his wife's assertion. "Say yes, Nicole, then we can all call you Nicki."

Dragging her mesmerized gaze from the lure of his blue eyes, Nicole glanced at the three expectant faces watching her. Laughing softly, she turned back to Josh. "Okay, J.B., Nicki it is," she agreed, extending her hand.

Nicole wasn't the only person in the room feeling slightly mesmerized. Just the sound of her laughter shook him to his foundations. As J.B. grasped her hand, he experienced a tingling sensation from his fingers to his shoulder that made him wonder if he were a victim of internal combustion. Staring at her from defensively hooded eyes, J.B. felt the moisture in his mouth drying rapidly.

Lord, she's exquisite! An emptiness yawned inside J.B.'s midsection as the thought filled his mind. The hollow feeling intensified as he released her hand. Shaken by a flood of emotions too complex to be examined in a sunny kitchen surrounded by friendly, interested faces, he worked his lips into the semblance of a smile.

"Nicki it is," J.B. repeated softly. Then, in an attempt to break the tension picking at his nerves, he shifted his gaze and grinned at Thack. "Did I hear somebody mention food and fresh coffee?" he asked.

"Plenty of both," Ellie announced. "If you all would sit down and give me some room," she directed, motioning to the oak kitchen table, "I'll serve it up."

A scrambling of settling into chairs ensued, and soon Ellie covered the table with all sorts of delicious food. Nicole took advantage of the general confusion to bring her wildly beating heart and activated imagination under control. The very fact that she found it necessary to bring her imagination under control rattled her.

Nicki. The echo of J.B.'s soft voice reverberated inside Nicole's head as she sampled a small portion of Ellie's special warm-weather salad, a cool and delicious concoction of molded Jell-O chock-full of walnuts, tiny pieces of crunchy apples, grated carrots and halved white grapes.

Nicki. The echo repeated as Nicole answered a barrage of questions from Barbara, in between tasty bites of a sinfully rich slice of chocolate cake, a specialty of the ex-model turned wife and mother.

Nicki. The echo resounded throughout Nicole's entire being as she cautiously sipped the steaming coffee in the earthenware mug Thack handed her.

Nicki. It was the recurring echo of her name that caused her imagination to take flight. As she ate, drank and tried to converse with at least a modicum of intelligence, Nicole quaked inwardly as she recalled the sound of her name on Josh Barnet's hard-looking lips, lips that for one mad instant she had craved to feel against her own. Nicole had known many men, of all ages, yet never had she experienced such a strong, physical response to a man, nor such a flight of erotic fancy.

"Nicki?"

Nicole jumped. She raised her eyes reluctantly to J.B. His lips moved, and there it was again. Slambang, her heart thumped, her pulses leaped, her lips burned with a need that was shocking in its intensity.

"I beg your pardon?" she murmured, unconsciously tasting his mouth with her avid gaze.

"I, uh, asked if you'd like more coffee." J.B.'s melodious voice cracked discordantly.

Nicole blinked to disperse the fog of sensuality clouding her senses. "Oh! Yes, thank you," she replied. *What is this?* she moaned silently.

What the hell is this? J.B. asked himself as he stared at the stream of coffee pouring into the mug he was gripping. The central air-conditioning unit kept the house comfortably cool, yet his forehead was damp with perspiration. He had begun to sweat moments ago while Nicki was staring at him or, more accurately, while she was staring at his mouth. And, what was worse, sweating wasn't the only way his body was reacting. As he carried the mug back to the table, J.B. prayed no one would notice anything.

Sitting down quickly, J.B. slid the mug across the table to Nicole, then avoided her eyes by staring into his own cooling coffee. The ploy was unsuccessful as an image of her formed in his mind. In fine detail he could see the lustrous sweep of her thick dark hair, the translucent flawlessness of her skin, the luring enticement of her sculpted lips. And then there were her eyes, dark brown with flecks of gold, their depths made darker by secrets, and pain, and a hunger J.B. instinctively knew she was unaware of.

Josh Barnet had more than a nodding acquaintance with secrets and pain and hunger. In fact, J.B. was an old pro at all three physical and emotional devils. He had challenged those particular devils and vanquished them. At least he'd believed he had. But that was before Nicole Vanzant stared at his mouth.

Sounding muted and faraway, the ongoing conversation swirled around him, heard yet not understood. Lifting the mug, J.B. swallowed the now tepid brew, grimacing as the liquid trickled down his dry throat. Thack was speaking, explaining the workings of the ranch to Nicole. Returning his attention to the table, J.B. glanced up over the rim of the mug and caught his breath sharply when his gaze tangled with Nicole's.

Her smile was fleeting but went straight to his senses, setting off electrical charges that exploded within him. Starting to sweat again, J.B. pulled his gaze from hers and looked down at the table. His glance brushed, then returned to the black-gloved hand resting on the polished oak surface. A sigh of acceptance whispered through his taut lips.

The palm inside that black glove was not damp with sweat. The fingers attached to the palm did not itch to stroke the faint scar that marred Nicole's satiny cheek. No, the hand encased in black leather was not of nature's design, not created of nerves, tendons, muscles, skin and bones. The hand hidden in black had been fashioned by man, of man-made properties. J.B. had lived with that somberly swathed hand for years. He'd believed he had learned to accept it as part of himself. He had been wrong.

Nicole's soft laughter crashed against J.B.'s eardrums—and his emotions. Through narrowed eyes he glared at the work-battered black leather. Resentment welled, tightening his chest and throat. Resentment against life, and fate, and the stupid circumstances that had left him with a stump below his left elbow.

Damn fate! J.B.'s cry went unheard by the others seated at the table but rang with anguished clarity inside his head.

Nicole didn't notice the black-gloved hand lying on the table. She hadn't, in fact, taken notice of it at all; she had been too overwhelmed at first by the tough look of him and later by the sheer beauty of his eyes to notice anything other than his height and leanness. In addition to his eyes, there was his deep, excitingly attractive voice that, each time he spoke, sent little tingles dancing madly along her spine. Was it any wonder she hadn't noticed his hand?

All the while Nicole had been responding to questions from Barbara and getting to know Thack and Ellie, both of whom she had already decided she was going to like, she had surreptitiously studied the blue-eyed, seductive-voiced, thin-lipped man seated opposite her at the gleaming table.

In a word, Josh Barnet fascinated Nicole Vanzant. That by itself astounded her—Nicole couldn't remember ever being fascinated by *any* man. Interested in, yes. But genuinely fascinated by? Never. And to actually crave to taste a man's mouth mere minutes after meeting him was a first Nicole felt positive she could have done without!

But she was fascinated by him, and she still did crave his mouth—like it or not. Now the bottom line of Nicole's problem was how she would deal with the craving and fascination should it continue throughout her entire visit at the ranch with Barbara and Thack.

Nicole unobtrusively squirmed on her thickly padded chair and laughed at whatever remark Thack had made, simply because Barbara and Ellie laughed. What in the world was the discussion about? Nicole hadn't a clue. Nor, in truth, did she care. At the moment she was too involved in admiring the way J.B.'s dark hair clung in thick waves to his head to be concerned with idle chatter. Black as a raven's feathers, shimmering with sparks of near blue in the sunlight, the silky strands of his hair caused an itch in her fingers—a desire to stroke and smooth. The urge was at once both frightening and exciting. It was also memory stirring.

A heaviness expanded in Nicole's chest, and her throat felt suddenly tight as a stinging, prickling sensation began at her temple and moved down the length of the faintly delineated scar. Now the urge compelling her fingers was to cover, conceal, the mark. Reality crashed in on her, and in a desperate bid to keep from screaming her pain and frustration aloud, Nicole forced her attention back to the conversation.

"Don't argue," Ellie said flatly, rising and beginning to clear the table. "I'll clean up. You get Nicole settled in."

Barbara opened her mouth to argue, but at that moment a demanding wail blared from an intercom set into the wall.

"You're being paged," Thack said, grinning rakishly at his wife. "You and Nicki go look after the princess, I'll help Aunt Ellie clean up in here."

"And I've got work to do," J.B. declared, scraping his chair back and getting to his feet.

It was then that Nicole noticed the strange way his arm hung at his side and the black glove that encased his hand.

Two

Alone in her room several hours later, Nicole smiled to herself as she moved back and forth between her suitcase on the bed and the open closet and dresser drawers. The smile was a result of the two hours she'd spent with Barbara and her daughter.

And what a little darling Rita was! Within seconds of entering the nursery, the baby had enslaved Nicole as completely as she had every other person on the Sharp property. Unused to children and their endearing ways, Nicole was doubly susceptible and lost from the very first owlish blink of Rita's big dark brown eyes.

Musing about one pair of dark eyes led to thoughts of another brighter pair, as deeply blue as the waters of mountain lakes, set in a face scored by life and the passage of time. The grooves bracketing J.B.'s face from his nostrils to the corners of his mouth spoke silently but eloquently of life lived and pain endured. Nicole couldn't help but question how much of that pain was directly related to the black-swathed hand hanging at his side.

Had J.B. been handicapped from birth? she wondered, shaking a skirt gently before clipping it to a hanger. Or had the handicap resulted from some sort of accident? Staring blankly at the floor, Nicole shivered; she understood the devastating effects of accidents. She lifted her hand to the scar on her face. Even after four years she could hear the blare of horns, the squeal of tires, the rending of metal and the screams of pain and terror. The screams had come from her throat; her companions in the car would never scream or know pain again.

Had J.B. suffered a similar experience? Caught in the relentless grip of nightmarish memory, Nicole was almost positive she didn't want to know J.B.'s story. Dealing with her own tale of horror was bad enough; she wasn't sure if she was up to dealing with yet another. However, the "almost" and "wasn't sure" in her thinking process gave her pause.

Why had she suddenly become interested in a man she didn't know? A frown drew a line between her eyebrows. She hadn't felt genuine interest in any man except her brother in years, ever since the accident. So why the interest now, in this particular man?

Scrupulously honest with herself, Nicole admitted to the instantaneous physical attraction she'd felt for J.B., which in itself was unusual. After years of almost total seclusion, was she now merely starved for male attention? Nicole frowned as she stashed away the empty flight bag and suitcase. Perhaps, but...

Nicole's train of thought was derailed by a soft tap on her door. Startled, she turned as Barbara called to her.

"Nicole, may I come in?"

"Yes, of course." Mentally shaking herself free of pointless introspection, she crossed the room, smiling as she swung the door open.

Barbara smiled hesitantly as she entered the room. "I didn't want to disturb you if you were resting." Her hazel eyes examined the evidence of weariness on Nicole's pale face. Her lips tightened as she noted the dark circles under Nicole's eyes and the way the scar, barely discernible most times, seemed to stand out in sharp contrast to the pallor of her delicate skin. "You should be resting," she said. "You look exhausted."

"I just finished unpacking and—"

"You should have left the unpacking," Barbara scolded. "I would have helped you with it later."

"I'm fine, Barbara, honestly." Moving her hand in a silent invitation for her friend to join her, Nicole turned to walk to the settee by the window. Seating herself in one plushly cushioned corner, Nicole smiled at Barbara's frown. "Don't fuss, please," she pleaded softly. "I had enough of that from my mother and Peter."

Sighing, Barbara dropped onto the settee. "Has it all been awful for you, Nicole?" she asked, tentatively broaching the subject of the accident's aftermath.

"For a while it was, yes," Nicole admitted. "I truly didn't want to live."

"Oh, Nicole, no!" Barbara protested.

"Oh, Barbara, yes," Nicole insisted candidly. "But fortunately, the will to live overcame the desire to give up." Nicole's smile was wry with self-knowledge. "I did a lot of thinking and maturing while I was hiding out at Peter's place in Maine.''

It was a second time Nicole had mentioned her brother, and Barbara knew she could no longer avoid the subject of her former lover. "How is Peter?" she asked, a trifle too brightly.

"I think you'd find him quite different," Nicole replied, laughing at her friend's skeptical expression. "Peter's in love," she explained.

"Peter! In love?" Barbara exclaimed, both astonished and amused. "I don't believe it! Who's the unlucky woman?" Her smile took the sting from the question.

Nicole smiled back in understanding; she knew her brother's reputation of uncaring casualness with women. Of course, since there was nothing uncaring or casual about him now, Nicole could smile easily.

"Her name is Patricia," Nicole said, her smile turning into laughter. "And she is cool, controlled and extremely beautiful." The gold flecks in her eyes sparkled. "And she has my oh-so-aloof brother running around in circles. And it couldn't happen to a more deserving man." She raised one eyebrow at Barbara. "I'm sure you'll agree."

Barbara nodded thoughtfully. "Peter did need some education on the female of the species."

Nicole laughed again. "Well, I suspect that school's been in session for him since the day he met Patricia." Her laughter subsided to a bemused smile. "They've only been married a little over a month, and I'm crazy about her already. And that's one of the reasons I accepted your invitation to spend the summer here." At Barbara's quizzical expression, Nicole explained, "I've been staying at Peter's town house in

Philadelphia since I decided to rejoin society. And since Peter has relocated to Philadelphia permanently—''

"Peter has moved his consulting business from New York to Philly?" Barbara interrupted in surprise.

"No." Nicole shook her head. "Peter has closed his consultancy office. He's concentrating all his time on saving the business Patricia's grandfather founded."

"Incredible!" Barbara looked stunned. "He really must be in love," she said in a tone of awe.

"Yes." Nicole's tone echoed Barbara's. "Patricia has definitely trained him."

"For a time there I had hoped that I might be the woman to..." Barbara's voice faded, then came back tinged with wry humor. "I was terribly smitten with Peter, you know."

"Yes." Nicole smiled. "And at the time I had hoped that you would be the one."

"But then I never would have met Thack." Barbara's eyes grew wide, and she laughed shakily. "I can't imagine existing without him now." She blinked at the sting of tears caused by the consideration. "I love Thack very much, Nicole," she said in a husky voice.

"I know." Nicole smiled and denied that the inner twinge she felt was envy for her happy friend. "I knew how deeply in love you both were the moment I saw you and Thack together."

Barbara grinned. "As blatant as all that, are we?"

"Yes." Nicole grinned back. "You adore Thack with your eyes, and he worships you with his." Her grin faded, and her expression became serious. "I like your Thack, Barbara. Your Aunt Ellie, too."

"And J.B.?" Barbara asked shrewdly.

"J.B.?" Nicole repeated in feigned confusion. "Why, I hardly know the man!" She expelled a flutter of nervous laughter.

"He's a good man, *Nicki*." A devilish smile tilted Barbara's lips as she emphasized the nickname.

"I'm sure he is, but—"

"And he deserves a good woman," Barbara went on implacably.

"I'm sure he does, but..." Beginning to feel smothered, Nicole let her voice fade.

"But he's handicapped?" Barbara asked, too gently.

Stunned by the censure hidden within Barbara's gentle tone, Nicole stared at her friend with eyes widened by shock. "Barbara!" she protested. "You know me better than that!"

"Actually, I don't," Barbara said, smiling to ease the sudden tension between them. "It's been a long time since our modeling days. We've both changed."

"Yes, we have." Nicole sighed, not in yearning for the old days but for the years in between. "You're a wife and mother now, and I'm—" she sighed again "—floundering around in nowhere land." Unaware of the forlorn image she created, she lowered her smarting eyes to her clenched hands.

Alarm flickered in Barbara's eyes. "No longer," she said, her tone determined. "There is no floundering allowed on the Sharp spread." She swallowed to relieve the sudden thickness in her throat when Nicole glanced up to offer a tired smile. "The first order of business is rest. You're practically out on your feet," she insisted when Nicole looked as if she might argue. Barbara shot a quick glance at the digital watch on her wrist. "To take advantage of the daylight hours, we have dinner late. You have plenty of time to have a relaxing bath and a nap.''

"Are you giving me general information or an order?'' Nicole's lips twitched with amusement.

"An order.'' Barbara laughed, leaning forward to brush her lips over Nicole's cheek before getting to her feet. "Thack tells me motherhood has made me bossy.'' She tossed a grin over her shoulder as she headed for the door. "We have the entire summer to get to know each other again. But right now you need some rest. So go to it,'' she advised, pausing as she pulled the door open. "I won't let you oversleep and miss Aunt Ellie's welcome dinner.'' Without waiting for a comment from Nicole, she stepped into the hallway and gently shut the door.

Nicole's vision blurred as she stared at the solid wood panel, and her soft lips quivered suspiciously. Then, blinking, she got up from the settee and began to undress. A half hour later, after soaking in a bath, she slipped a soft, silky nightgown over her head, then slid between pale rose percale sheets. A sigh of sheer bliss whispering through her lips, Nicole closed her eyes, positive she'd be asleep in seconds. She was right; sleep claimed her mere moments after her heavy eyelids drifted shut....

The terrain was rough and uneven and dotted by large rocks and boulders that seemed as if they'd been flung to the ground by an angry deity at the beginning of time.

Time. *Time.* Time was of the essence, and it was running out for someone very important to Nicole. Her throat dry and raw, her chest constricted and burning, Nicole forced her leaden legs to move one more step, then two, then three. The sky was over-

cast, robbing the night of the illuminating light from
the moon and the stars. Warmth had deserted the land
with the setting sun. A chill breeze soughed mourn-
fully through the trees, arousing shivers of cold and
fear throughout her body. Nicole knew she couldn't
stop, not even for breath. She was the only one who
knew, the only one who could help.

Help. Dear Lord, why didn't someone come looking for her to help? He would die without help.
Somehow, by instinct or intuition or something, Nicole knew that he would die unless he received help
soon. And she was tired, growing weaker with each
dragging step. Why wasn't someone helping her?

Then someone was there. Nicole could feel the
presence. Silent, darker than the night, more terrify-
ing than the chill, moaning wind. He was closing in on
her—she could smell the sweaty odor of horse and
man, could hear the ring of shod hooves on stone.
Hand pressed to her throat, she opened her mouth to
scream. A voice called out before a sound could pass
her lips.

"Nicole! Wake up!"

Nicole bolted upright on the bed, her eyes wide and
searching, her breath coming in short gasps. Very real,
very frightening, the dream clung to her mind like a
sticky web.

"Honey, are you all right?" The hand that touched
her arm was as gentle as the voice that swept away the
clinging strands of the nightmare. Nicole focused her
clearing vision on hazel eyes darkened by concern.

"Oh, Barbara." Relief shivered through Nicole. "I
was dreaming."

"I know. I could hear you whimpering from the
hallway." Sitting on the bed, Barbara stroked Ni-

cole's arm comfortingly, as she would a frightened child. "Do you get nightmares about the accident?" she asked with soft compassion.

"The accident?" Nicole frowned; she hadn't dreamed about the accident in over three years. "No." She shook her head, then glanced over at the window. Dusk was settling gently onto the Texas hill country. "I dreamed I was out there," she said, her tone reedy. "It was so very dark, and I was alone and frightened. But I had to find someone, someone who needed help to survive." Her voice grew strained. "Then there was someone there, a man, a dark man and...and..." Her voice deserted her.

"You screamed," Barbara inserted soothingly. "It was only a dream, Nicole. Probably brought on by exhaustion." A smile tugged at her lips. "And possibly the wild look of the landscape unconsciously preyed on your mind as you drove here today."

"Possibly," Nicole murmured, not believing it for a second. In truth, she had been impressed by the untamed look of the countryside, but she had in no way felt intimidated; the Texas hill country was no more forbidding than sections of the rugged Maine coast, just different. Drawing her gaze from the window, she gave Barbara a crooked smile. "I did sleep, though," she said dryly.

"Good." Barbara smiled her relief. "Now that you're rested, are you hungry?"

"Famished." Nicole laughed, realizing it was true. "Is dinner ready?" she asked hopefully, noting Barbara's casual attire of free-flowing pants in a silky material and loose pullover top with a Mexican motif embroidered across the front in vibrant colors.

"It will be in a few minutes. Thack and J.B. are cleaning up even as we speak." Grinning, Barbara slid from the bed and strolled to the door. "Don't fuss. We only get dressed up for dinner when we have company."

Barbara's parting remark infused Nicole with a warmth that chased the last lingering chill left over from the dream. Grateful for being considered more family than company, she hummed to herself as she stepped into lightweight beige slacks and topped them with a silk knit sweater in an amber shade that enhanced the gold flecks in her eyes. Her makeup was applied sparingly except for the covering she lavished on the scar. After brushing gold eye shadow over each eyelid and adding a dash of copper gloss to her lips, she was ready to face almost anything. Only to herself would Nicole admit that the "almost" included one tough-looking dude named Josh Barnet.

That evening Nicole strode unerringly along the hallway, softly illuminated by brass wall sconces. Admiring the decor of combined Mexican and traditional Western, she followed the sound of muted conversation from the living room. Growing uneasy, she strained to hear the low exciting voice that would signal the presence of Thack's foreman. Before she had set foot in the foyer, Nicole had identified Ellie's rather caustic tone, Thack's laconic drawl and Barbara's laughter. There was not a hint of the deep voice that, for reasons she preferred not to examine, filled her with a confusing sense of both trepidation and anticipation.

Startled by the moisture on her palms and feeling a chill feathering down her spine, Nicole paused in the wide doorway to the living room. She swiftly surveyed the spacious room, then released a sigh of relief. The rawly intimidating, tough-looking foreman wasn't there. But before her sigh was fully spent, Nicole felt an odd tingle at her nape. The cause of the tingle made her jump by speaking close to her left ear.

"Go on in, the booze is fine," J.B. paraphrased, amusement woven through his sexy voice.

Stiffening, Nicole spun to face him, the gold flecks in her eyes flashing with annoyance. "You startled me!" she accused him, appalled by the sensations rioting through her nervous system. The apologetic smile he offered her accelerated the riot into a full-scale debacle.

"Fair exchange," J.B. muttered. "You startled me, too."

Not sure she had heard him correctly, Nicole was about to question his cryptic mutter when Barbara spied them.

"Well, it's about time you two got here," she scolded teasingly. "I'm on my second glass of wine!"

"Not to mention on her way to being sloshed," Thack said dryly. "If we don't soon shovel some food into this woman, she'll be out for the count."

"Thackery Sharp! I resent that remark." Barbara's laughing hazel eyes belied the scowl on her lovely face. "I am perfectly capable of handling two glasses of wine."

Sauntering to the small credenza bar in a corner, Thack glanced over his shoulder and arched his eyebrows at his wife. "That's right," he agreed in a deceptively soothing tone, a glint of deviltry lighting his brown eyes. "It's me you can't handle."

Thack's observation elicited a yelp followed by a tirade from Barbara. A smile relieving the tension zinging through Nicole, she entered the room. Exchanging smiles with Ellie, Nicole accepted the wine Thack offered her without pausing in his relentless teasing of his wife. Never having been exposed to it, Nicole was utterly fascinated by the good-natured banter between a man and a woman so obviously in love. A smile of contentment curving her lips, she sat back in an overstuffed chair, thoroughly enjoying their loving word battle.

J.B. sat back to enjoy, also, but not the verbal thrust and parry between Thack and Barbara. After nine months of daily contact, J.B. had grown accustomed to the laughing, loving interaction. Most times it amused him. But there were instances where the affectionate play between the two people he loved most in the world—other than his family—gave J.B. a yawning sense of loss.

That evening J.B. didn't hear the echo of marital success. J.B. was too involved in enjoying the delectable woman seated across the room from him. The perfection of her beauty continued to astound him. Her allure continued to arouse him. That evening, sipping cold beer from a frosted mug, J.B. savored the waves of sensual heat coursing through his body and decided to grill Thack about his lovely guest the first moment he could get his boss alone.

Nicki. J.B. rolled the nickname around in his mind as he sketched her much too slender body with a hooded gaze. Allowing his imagination to run free, J.B. envisioned himself stripping her of the elegant simplicity of her clothes, along with all civilized restraint. Making a game of guessing what she was wearing under the circumspect slacks and sweater, he decided to partially cover her in an enticing lacy teddy.

What the hell? J.B. shrugged mentally. It was his game, wasn't it? And he did have a thing for lacy teddies.

His eyes narrowing to mere slits, J.B. could actually see her, stretched out across his bed. And, too thin or not, he decided she looked mighty enticing in a lacy teddy. And he sure as hell couldn't resist the temptation of a pliant Nicole!

Pursuing his game, J.B. felt a sharp thrill as he pictured his hand slowly guiding one lacy strap over the satin skin of her shoulder, exposing one pink-tipped breast to his hot gaze and even hotter mouth. Closing his eyes completely, he could feel the puckered texture of that tight, hard bud, could taste the scented sweetness of her skin. A groan swelled in his throat, then filled his mouth. J.B. denied the sound passage by clamping his lips together. But damn, she was so soft, so deliciously sweet!

Suddenly parched, J.B. took an overlarge swallow of beer and choked as the cold brew rushed down his throat. His eyes sprang open, and coughing violently, he proceeded to splash beer over the rim of the mug and onto his jeans.

"What the hell are you doing, ol' son, trying to drown yourself?" Moving with astonishing speed for such a big man, Thack was across the room and pounding on J.B.'s back in an instant.

"J.B., are you all right?" Right on her husband's heels, Barbara retrieved the dangerously wobbling mug as she peered with concern into his reddening face.

"Yeah," J.B. grunted between bouts of coughing. "Unless you count feeling like an idiot. I, er, started to doze off with beer in my mouth." He said the first thing that came into his mind, then cursed himself for sounding even more idiotic.

"Well, if that's not the most ridiculous thing I ever heard!" Ellie exclaimed, the tension easing from her concerned expression.

Although she kept it to herself, Nicole agreed with the older woman. Who in the world ever heard of dozing off holding a mouthful of any kind of liquid? Perhaps her first impression about Thack's finding J.B. in a cave had come close to the mark; falling asleep while drinking was hardly the norm for a civilized man. It if came to that, idiot got close to the mark, as well.

And attractive?

And exciting?

And sexy?

Nicole fidgeted as the questions chased one another through her mind. Frowning, she attempted to banish the queries. In defiance they bounced right back, demanding a response.

So, okay, the man was attractive—in a rough sort of way.

And, maybe, he was exciting—probably because he was so very different from any other man she'd ever met.

But was he sexy? Nicole reluctantly shifted her gaze to where J.B. now stood, wiping the wet spot on his jeans with a paper cocktail napkin. Was the man sexy? God, yes! she thought, shaken by the chill followed by intense heat that went coursing through her body.

Unable to move or draw her gaze away from him, Nicole sat shivering, a silent captive to his every move. Then, as if feeling her stare, J.B. became still and slowly raised his eyes to hers. Nicole's heartbeat slowed, then increased to a frightening thunder as she gazed into his eyes. She felt as if she were flying in a sapphire-blue infinity. Were there silver lights in that density of blue? Or were they stars? At that moment Nicole didn't care. All she asked was the privilege to free-fall forever in the depths of sapphire blue. The privilege was denied her by the down-to-earth voice of Barbara's aunt.

"J.B., I suggest you go change into other pants, instead of wasting energy wiping those jeans with that napkin." Turning away, she started for the kitchen. "Meanwhile, I'm going to put dinner on the table. I don't know about the rest of you folks," she shot back over her shoulder, "but I'm hungry."

"Better hop to it, friend," Thack advised in an amused drawl. "You know Ellie. If you're not back double-quick, she'll serve you cold shoulder with a sharp tongue for supper."

"I heard that, Thackery Sharp!" Ellie shouted from the kitchen. "And he's damn straight, J.B., so get it in gear."

Thack smirked.

Barbara smothered a burst of laughter behind her hand.

J.B. sent a narrow-eyed glare toward the kitchen but then moved to obey the bossy command. He had taken only three steps when Ellie's voice again rang through the room.

"And don't be aimin' dirty looks at my back, either!"

Muttering "Cranky old woman," J.B. strode from the room, followed by a chuckle from Thack and an explosion of laughter from Barbara.

Not certain how to react, Nicole merely stared in surprise at her laughing host and hostess. As her amusement subsided, Barbara noticed the expression of bemused curiosity on her friend's face. The look Barbara and Thack shared spoke of near perfect accord.

"Don't let the heated talk throw you, Nicki," Thack said, a soft smile tilting his lips.

"Don't Ellie and J.B. get along very well?" Nicole swallowed the sigh that followed the question. She had thought she was leaving this type of family squabbling behind in Philadelphia. After witnessing her brother and mother snipe continually at each other, Nicole was fed up to the teeth with internal family dissension.

"Not get along!" Barbara exclaimed. "Aunt Ellie and J.B. are crazy about each other!"

"But—" That was as far as Nicole got.

"And they are both down-to-earth straight shooters," Thack inserted. "Ellie and J.B. understand one another."

"Which gives us the freedom to say what's on our minds," Ellie clarified from the dining room archway. "It's a nice, warm feeling, having a friend like that," she added softly. Then, her tone brisk, she said, "Supper's on the table. It's time to eat. With or without the hombre."

Hombre? Nicole frowned, but before she had a chance to ask any questions, the man under discussion spoke from the double doorway.

"The hombre's here, you West Texas renegade."

Appalled by the name-calling, Nicole began to stiffen but relaxed again when Ellie gave a bark of laughter.

"And don't you forget it, cowboy," she said, motioning to them to go to the table. "I may not have been born here, but I'd sunk my roots in West Texas before you ever saw the light of day."

"Braggy old broad, isn't she?" J.B. observed mildly, following Ellie into the room to then hold her chair for her with an endearing courtesy. As she sat down, he leaned over her shoulder to tease softly, "If you weren't so prickly tongued, I might propose marriage."

"And drop dead from a heart attack when I accepted," Ellie retorted, shooing him away with an impatient wave of her hand. "Now park it so we can eat. I didn't cook this food to let it get cold on the table."

The banter continued throughout the meal, which Nicole decided she wouldn't have missed for tea with the governor of the state, any state. Besides her first taste of chicken fried steak with milky pan gravy ladled over homemade biscuits, she had her first example of congenial family life. Conversation was lively, at times even hilarious, and Nicole soaked it up like a dried-out sponge. More accustomed to meals eaten in solitary silence, or on occasion at her parents' home, listening to her father play referee between her acidic mother and her cynical brother, Nicole thoroughly enjoyed the food served in an atmosphere of relaxed camaraderie. She even enjoyed the tingle of apprehensive anticipation that slid deliciously down her spine every time her glance collided with J.B.'s.

They were still at the table, lingering over coffee, when Rita made a squalling demand via the intercom for her mother's attention.

"You see how considerate my daughter is?" Barbara grinned at Nicole as she slid her chair away from the table. "She's probably starving, waiting all this time for me to finish my dinner." She transferred the grin to her aunt as she walked to the archway. "She's also getting me out of helping clear away again."

"May I come up to the nursery later?" Nicole called after her.

"Certainly," Barbara called back. "You can help me give Rita her bath."

Delighted with the invitation, Nicole jumped up and began clearing the table; she had never given a baby a bath, and the prospect was intriguing.

Already on her feet and gathering dishes, Ellie paused to level a cool look on the two men. "Well, are you going to help or clear out of here and give us some working room?" she asked tartly.

The men moved in unison, both in Barbara's wake.

"I'm going to visit my daughter," Thack said.

"I've got work to do," J.B. declared.

"Oh, for the easy life of a man," Ellie taunted to their retreating backs. "Really, both Thack and J.B. work long, hard hours," she said to Nicole the moment the men were out of hearing. "Thack hung around today because he wanted to welcome you. Won't see near as much of him tomorrow." Hands laden with dishes, Ellie started for the kitchen. "And probably even less of J.B."

Since the man unnerved her, Nicole should have felt infinitely relieved. Following Ellie into the kitchen, she wondered why she didn't.

Three

———

Less than a half hour later Nicole tiptoed into the nursery and stopped dead in her tracks, mouth gaping and eyes widening at the sight that met her gaze.

Sitting on a rocker in a dimly lit corner of the room, J.B. was bent protectively over the baby he cradled in one arm, feeding her a bottle with his ungloved right hand. An expression of tenderness gentled his harshly defined features. A bemused smile softened his thin lips.

"Sure," he murmured, his beautiful voice low and crooning. "It's no wonder you were wailing for your mama. Doesn't anybody around here feed you?" His movements economical, he dexterously shifted the infant to his shoulder, then stroked her tiny back with his broad palm. "Well, not to worry, little love, the hombre's here to take care of you." As if to punctuate J.B.'s assurance, the baby burped the moment he stopped speaking.

Hombre again? A tiny frown marred the softness of Nicole's expression. Didn't hombre simply mean *man*? Frowning, Nicole studied the intimidating man who was handling the infant with the ease of an experienced father. The thought aroused speculation. Was J.B. an experienced father? Nicole knew virtually nothing about him and realized that he could very well be married. The sudden sharp pang that twisted inside her chest startled Nicole. Unnerved by her strange reaction to the idea of J.B. with a woman, Nicole sighed with relief when Thack quietly entered the room and smiled at her.

"Barbara sent me to find you," he whispered. "J.B. and I agreed to take over with Rita tonight to give you and Barb a chance to spend some time alone together." Thack grinned. "She said to tell you the wine is chilled. She's waiting for you in the living room."

"Thanks, Thack." Acting on impulse, Nicole gave him a quick kiss on the cheek. "You're special."

"You're pretty special, too," Thack drawled. "Now get out of here. I'll see you tomorrow."

Smiling, Nicole turned to glance at the baby before leaving the room. Rita was contentedly finishing her bottle. The expression on the face of the man cradling her tiny body was anything but content. J.B.'s features were set in a disapproving frown, and his hooded eyes were glaring directly at Nicole.

Shaken by his inexplicable coldness, Nicole returned his stare for an instant, then she slipped silently from the room. What had she done to earn J.B.'s censure? she wondered as she made her way to the living room. Surely he wasn't annoyed because she had walked into the nursery and caught him in a display of tenderness toward Rita? The thought deepened her frown. Was J.B. afraid he had blown his tough image? Nicole was still frowning as she entered the living room.

"Good heavens!" Barbara exclaimed. "Why the scowl? You look like a cloud about to rain on someone."

Dropping onto the chair opposite her friend, Nicole smiled wryly. "I'm trying to figure out your foreman," she explained.

"Oh, well, that clears up everything." Barbara laughed. "Figuring out J.B. is about as simple as working a Chinese puzzle." Shrugging, she leaned over the low table in front of her chair. On the table were two tulip-shaped glasses and a bottle of an excellent Chardonnay. After filling both glasses, Barbara handed one to Nicole. "Now what is it you'd like explained about J.B.?" she asked, lifting her glass in a silent salute.

"The use of the term 'hombre,' for starters," Nicole replied, returning the silent toast. "Doesn't the word simply mean 'man'?"

"Hmmm, literally yes," Barbara said, grinning. "But in J.B.'s case it means a great deal more. You see, before either Aunt Ellie or I ever met him, Thack described J.B. to us as being one tough hombre. And as that description has proved to be absolutely on target, first Aunt Ellie, then Thack and I got into the habit of calling him 'the hombre.' Now he occasionally refers to himself by the name." Barbara sipped the wine and sighed in appreciation of its superior flavor. "I suspect that before long you'll be calling him 'hombre,' too."

I seriously doubt it. Nicole kept the observation to herself, letting a "Hmmm" suffice for a response. Running the tip of one slender finger around the rim of the wineglass, she said softly, "How did he lose his arm?"

"In the line of duty," Barbara replied in a flat voice. "Why? Does the idea of the artificial appendage bother you?"

Startled, Nicole glanced up, eyes wide with confusion. "Bother me," she repeated. "In what way?"

Barbara hesitated, then said bluntly, "Do you find it repulsive?"

"Of course not!" Nicole denied fervently. "Why would you even think—"

"Some people are repulsed by it, you know," Barbara cut in. "The sight of it makes them uncomfortable or something."

"Yes." Nicole nodded as she lifted her finger from the rim of the glass to stroke the hairline scar on her cheek. "I'm well aware of the reactions to disfigurement."

"Nicole, you are no more disfigured than J.B.!" Barbara said sharply. "Why, the scar is barely noticeable. And if there are those who are uncomfortable because of it, I'd say the problem is theirs, not yours."

"Perhaps," Nicole murmured, neither agreeing nor disagreeing with her friend. "At any rate, what I told you earlier was true. J.B.'s handicap doesn't bother me." Her smile was wry. "Actually, I find the man himself rather intimidating."

Barbara laughed. "I know what you mean. I had the same reaction the first time I met him."

Nicole sat up alertly. Had Barbara experienced the same kind of immediate sexual attraction to J.B. on her introduction to the laconic foreman? she wondered uneasily. Barbara's chuckle snagged Nicole's attention. Her subsequent remark set Nicole's mind at ease.

"To be perfectly honest, the man scared the hell out of me on first sight."

Nicole sighed her relief. "Is he married?" she probed.

"No," Barbara murmured and took a sip of wine. "But he really should be," she continued after swallowing. "He's a terrific man. And he loves children," she added, unaware of Nicole's prior knowledge to that effect. "You should see him with Rita."

"I have," Nicole murmured, smiling softly. "I was in the nursery when Thack tracked me down. J.B. was feeding a bottle to Rita. I was amazed by his gentleness. Seems strange he never married and had children of his own."

Barbara's eyes narrowed in anger, and her lips twisted as if from a bitter taste. "He was engaged. The woman dumped him after the accident."

Nicole's smile vanished, and her eyes widened in shock. "But why?"

"I suppose she didn't consider J.B. a *whole* man any longer," Barbara said tiredly. "Thack didn't tell me much, but I didn't have to be clairvoyant to figure out that the woman broke their engagement while J.B. was still in the hospital."

"Oh, no," Nicole murmured.

"Oh, yes," Barbara insisted, the bitter smile flicking over her lips again. "Apparently the gutless fool couldn't stand the sight of his bandaged stump. She fell apart and ran. She nearly destroyed J.B. in the process."

Nicole sipped her wine, then stared into the glass, imagining the trauma inflicted upon an injured, weakened J.B. by the woman he loved and trusted. The blow would have been devastating, she decided, for a man as proud as J.B. obviously was. "And there has been no other woman?" she asked softly, glancing up at her friend.

"Oh, there have been several women." Barbara smiled sadly. "All of them brief encounters of the physical kind. J.B. treats women very well, but he never lets any of them get too close." She sighed heavily. "It's a shame, really. He's a genuinely good man, with a lot to give to a deep relationship. But he's gun-shy now and no longer offering anything more than friendship or a few nights of mutually shared pleasure."

A silence settled in the room as both women concentrated on their wine and their own thoughts. Barbara's thoughts were all of gentle compassion for the tough-looking man who had become her good friend. Nicole's thoughts, while including compassion for J.B., were less gentle and fraught with an uneasy sense of impending emotional turmoil.

Having completely lost her head and made an absolute mess of her life over one man, Nicole wasn't looking for any sort of relationship with another, let alone a brief encounter of the physical kind. And yet there was something about J.B. that caused an aching yearning inside her. And the ache had a lot more to do with the physical than compassion—and Nicole knew it.

Uncomfortable with the direction of her thoughts, Nicole tossed back the last swallow of wine in her glass, then leaned forward to hand it to Barbara.

"May I have a refill?" she asked softly, breaking the lengthy silence.

Barbara blinked, then laughed self-consciously. "Yes, of course!" Her lips curved into a rueful smile. "I'm sorry if I put a damper on the evening."

Nicole managed a shrug. "I asked," she said, then smiled. "I like your family, Barbara," she went on, obviously changing the subject. Nicole glanced around the large, comfortable room. "And I like your home." Her lips slanted in a wry smile. "In truth, I envy you," she admitted candidly.

"Thank you, I rather like them, too." Barbara returned Nicole's smile before giving way to the frown tugging at her lips. "But why envy me? Why haven't you started a family of your own?"

Nicole shifted her shoulders in a helpless shrug. "I haven't met any man I cared to spend a few hours with, let alone starting a family."

"Are you still grieving for—"

"No." Nicole answered before Barbara could say the man's name. Lowering her eyes from Barbara's direct gaze, Nicole stared blankly into the golden wine in her glass. How very like Barbara to slice right to the point, to almost cut through the years, she thought partly amused, partly chagrined.

"Nicole?" Barbara said hesitantly. "I'm sorry if I struck a nerve."

Nicole sighed. Was she that sensitive? That raw? Yes, of course she was, she acknowledged wearily. Hadn't she refused to discuss *him* with anyone, even the assortment of analysts her mother had dragged her to, all this time? Didn't she, even now, shy away from thinking his name? Drawing in a deep breath, Nicole forced her mind to form his name. Jason. His name was, had been, Jason Norwich. And maybe the time for purging was long overdue, she decided suddenly. And who better than Barbara to purge to? Barbara had always understood, or at least had tried to. Raising her eyes from the glass, Nicole met Barbara's concerned gaze.

"No, I'm not still grieving for Jason." Having cleared the hurdle of saying his name aloud, Nicole's voice gained strength. "I never was honestly grieving," she confessed. "Not for Jason or my lost career as a model."

"But, then..." Barbara began, shaking her head slowly in confusion.

"Why did I withdraw, hide in Peter's cottage along the Maine coast?" Nicole finished for Barbara. "Because I was trying to come to terms, live with the guilt I was feeling," she explained when Barbara nodded.

"Guilt!" Barbara exclaimed, sitting bolt upright in her chair. "Nicole, you were asleep in the back seat of that car! You were in no way responsible for that accident. Why would you feel guilty?" she demanded, coming to Nicole's defense, as she always had years before. "Dammit, Nicole, Jason was driving that car, not you!"

"And Jason was flying pretty high," Nicole said quietly.

"I know that, but—"

"I should have known it, too." Nicole cut off the beginning of Barbara's argument. Suddenly dry, she gulped her wine and watched as realization dawned on Barbara's face. "I had known for over a month before the accident that Jason had long since passed the experimental stage with drugs."

"But why blame yourself?" Barbara said slowly. "Unless you were..."

Nicole smiled wryly as Barbara's voice faded. "No, I wasn't into the scene," she answered the unfinished question. "Not even experimentally, although I realized later that everyone believed I was playing around with that particular fire." Lifting her glass, she drank deeply, thirstily. "To tell you the truth, I've always been scared to try drugs." She tilted the glass at Barbara, adding, "I rarely even indulge in drinking, except for the occasional glass of wine before or with dinner."

"I know," Barbara murmured. "At least I did know—before you seemed to get caught up with the party crowd. But I still don't understand why you blamed yourself for the accident."

"For the very reason that I hadn't indulged that night," Nicole explained. "I had spent the entire evening sipping one wine spritzer and nagging Jason to take me back to Manhattan, even though I knew he wanted to stay at the party." The memory of that horrible night closed in on Nicole. Her throat tight, she continued rawly, "But even then I failed to realize why he insisted on staying." Nicole sighed. "I suppose I simply didn't want to face the fact of his dependence on it. At any rate, I insisted on returning to the city. After the accident I felt that if I hadn't made such a fuss about leaving, Jason and the other man in the car would still be alive."

Though it appeared that she wanted to interrupt several times during Nicole's explanation, Barbara managed to hold her tongue until Nicole finished. Then she exploded.

"Nicole, that's absolutely ridiculous!"

Nicole shrugged. "I know that—now. But I spent long, agonizing months coming to that conclusion."

"You loved Jason very much?" Barbara asked softly.

"No," Nicole said starkly. "For a while, at the very beginning, I thought I did. But I realize now that I was merely infatuated with him. He was so utterly different from any man I had ever met."

"I'll say," Barbara observed in a dry tone, remembering the breathtaking good looks of the ultrawith-it man who had breezed into Nicole's life and swept her off her feet and into the glittering, tawdry world of drugs, booze and all-night parties. "He was a mite too different for my tastes."

"But then," Nicole murmured, "you always did have more sense than I did."

"My New England upbringing," Barbara drawled, then added, "And you were so unbelievably innocent."

"The product of an overprotective older brother," Nicole said, shaking her head in wonder at her own gullibility, even after several years of modeling. "I learned the hard way that we do indeed pay for our mistakes."

"But you have finally resolved the guilt feelings?" Barbara asked hopefully.

"Oh, yes." Nicole's smile was free of strain. "It took a long time, too long a time—" her smile slanted sardonically "—and I realize now that I should have opened up to the assortment of analysts, or at least one of them. But the guilt is resolved. Now all I have to do is piece my life back together again."

Barbara fidgeted with her glass's slender stem, then asked tentatively, "You're going to try to go back to modeling?"

"Good Lord, no!" Nicole stated vehemently. "I'm well out of that competitive scramble, and I know it." She frowned. "Do you miss it?"

"Not me." Barbara shook her head sharply. "As the saying goes, I may be crazy, but I'm sure not nuts! Other than doing one job I figured I owed my agent and myself, I chucked it without a twinge when Thack asked me to marry him. And I wouldn't trade what I've got now for the promise of eternal youth and my face smiling from the cover of every magazine going."

"Good for you."

Both women jumped, their heads turning at the sound of the attractive male voice. J.B. stood in the center of the double doorway, his expression somber, his eyes hooded.

"J.B.!" Barbara exclaimed. "Are you trying to give me a heart attack?"

"Sorry," he murmured, strolling into the room. As he drew closer, Nicole thought he didn't sound sorry; he didn't look it, either. A hint of a smile played over his lips. "I was on my way out," he said. "I just wanted to say good-night."

Out? Nicole frowned mentally and slid a glance at her watch. It was almost midnight, and he was going out? Out where? Telling herself to mind her own business, she looked up in time to catch him responding to Barbara's offer of a drink.

"No, thanks. I'm headed for the sack. Four-thirty comes mighty early." He gave Barbara one of his state-of-the-art smiles. "I'd have been out of here long ago, but I dozed off in the rocker. Thack packed it in an hour ago, and Rita's sleeping like a professional. Thought you might want to know." Pivoting, he sauntered toward the doorway. "Night, ladies," he called softly over his shoulder. A moment later the front door shut with a gentle click.

"Who was that masked man?" Nicole asked. Her feigned tone of awe had not been difficult to achieve.

"I'm not sure, but I think he has something to do with riding a white horse and saving people from themselves." Barbara chuckled. "Do you suppose he was trying to tell us something?" She worked her expression into a confused frown.

"You mean like lay off the sauce and go to bed?" Nicole fluttered her eyelashes over innocently widened eyes.

"Could be." Barbara nodded sagely. "It's probably very good advice. We have all summer to talk. We really don't have to do it all the first night you're here."

"One question?" Nicole pleaded, yawning as she got to her feet.

"Of course!" Barbara paused in the act of collecting empty glasses and the almost empty wine bottle. "What do you want to know?"

"J.B. said he was going out, then he said he was going to bed." Nicole frowned. "Did I miss something in between?"

Barbara grinned sleepily. "No. J.B. doesn't live here in the house," she explained. "He doesn't even have meals with us as a rule. He has his own place on the property. I'll show it to you tomorrow." She smothered a yawn with the back of her hand. "But right now I'm for bed."

"And me," Nicole agreed, trailing Barbara into the kitchen. "Is there anything I can do to help?"

"No." Barbara shook her head. "You go on up. I'm only going to rinse these glasses." Setting the glasses and bottle on the countertop, she then turned to embrace Nicole. "I'm so glad you decided to accept our invitation. Sleep well. I'll see you—" she broke off to step back and smile "—whenever you decide to surface. I want you to feel at home here. But I also want you to remember that you're on vacation. Come and go as you please."

"Thank you, Barbara." Nicole's throat felt tight, and her eyes misted. Reaching out, she squeezed Barbara's hand. "I'm glad I came. Good night." Blinking against a surge of tears, Nicole turned and walked out of the kitchen.

"Good night, Nicki."

A wobbly smile curved Nicole's lips as Barbara's soft call caught up to her in the foyer. Nicki. Yes, she rather liked the nickname, she mused, slowly climbing the stairs. As to the man who had bestowed the name upon her... Nicole's thoughts jumbled as an image of Josh Barnet filled her mind. Playing havoc with her breathing process, the image stayed with her as she prepared for bed and grew even stronger after she had slipped between the sheets.

Josh Barnet.

Nicole shivered deliciously as she repeated his name to herself. "Josh Barnet."

Merely murmuring his name aloud intensified the shiver and clarified the image in her mind. As clearly as if he stood before her in the blaze of the bright Texas sunlight, Nicole could see the roughly chiseled planes and angles of his face, the startling beauty of his blue eyes, the strange lure of his mouth.

What was it about his mouth?

Shifting restlessly, Nicole tried to avoid the inner question but it persisted. What was it about his mouth? Her heartbeat kicked into high gear, her breathing grew shallow, her lips burned.

Tentatively, almost fearfully, Nicole slid the tip of her tongue along her hot lower lip. It was ridiculous. It was beyond comprehension. It was as plain as the nose on her face. What was it about Josh Barnet's mouth? Nicole shuddered, then faced the answer. She wanted it.

"Oh, God!"

Rolling over, Nicole buried her face in the pillow. She was just getting her head together, just beginning to glimpse daylight at the end of what had proved to be a very dark tunnel. The absolute last thing she wanted or needed was a reactivated libido!

But there it was, doing cartwheels of joy at being sprung from solitary confinement, bubbling riotously through her body, alerting her senses, heating her blood, telling her secrets she'd prefer not to know.

"Damn!"

Gritting her teeth, Nicole flopped onto her back and lay rigid, glaring at the ceiling, her mind spinning with questions. Why? Why here? Why now? Why him? And then one final question. Why hadn't she simply stayed in Philadelphia, where she was safe?

Safe? Nicole frowned. She had literally spent the past few years as safely as was humanly possible while still staying alive. Safe had been hiding in a haven on the Maine coast, eating meals for one, taking solitary walks along the rugged coastline, slipping into bed alone as she had moments before. Safe was self-examination and doubt, and loneliness, and celibacy. Living safe was barely living at all; it was simply existing. Safe included boredom and excluded excitement. Did she honestly want to continue playing it safe?

On the other hand... Nicole caught her bottom lip between her teeth as memory replayed the single alternative she had experienced.

Deciding against attending college, Nicole had begun modeling professionally the summer after she had graduated from high school. Because of the near perfection of her features, her tall, slim body and the unaffected, natural grace of her movements, her rise to fame had been meteoric. Yet even with the excitement generated by the sometimes fawning attention she'd received, the looming presence of her brother in the background had kept her safe. That is, until she met Jason Norwich.

The adored only son of a wealthy family, at twenty-five Jason was magazine-cover handsome, worldly wise and experienced in the ways of pleasing a woman, most especially a woman he wanted to bed. And from the moment they met, Jason made it no secret that he not only wanted but fully intended to take Nicole to his bed.

Flattered, flustered and excited by his bold advances, Nicole had fallen head over heels into his arms and into his bed...in that order. Though practiced and passionate, Jason's lovemaking left a lot to be desired. At the time, vaguely dissatisfied and not sure why, Nicole blamed herself, her innocence. It was much later, while she prowled the rocky, wind-tossed Maine coast, that she questioned her acceptance of her own inadequacy. Of course, by then it was too late. Nicole had blamed herself—for just about everything.

Nicole's infatuation with Jason lasted for all of two months, yet she continued to see him, accompany him to parties that grew steadily wilder and more frightening.

As late as the fateful night on which they had gone to that party on Long Island, Nicole had coaxed and threatened and begged him to admit himself for detoxification. Jason had merely smiled his charming, boyish smile, caressed her cheek with his fingers and told her not to worry, that he could handle it. He had actually convinced her he'd not indulged his habit the night of the party, too. Oh, yes, he could handle it. Jason had handled the expensive sports car directly into the path of a sixteen wheeler. Jason and a friend of his who'd asked to ride back with them were sitting in the front seat. The men were killed instantly. Curled up on the small back seat asleep, Nicole had escaped death but had sustained multiple injuries and scars, both inside and out, that she would carry for the rest of her life.

It had required years of solitude and soul-searching for Nicole to resolve her feelings of guilt—guilt for getting involved with him in the first place; guilt for her inability to convince him to seek help; guilt for not realizing his condition that night; and finally, guilt for allowing him to drive. Years and years of guilt for three brief months of unsafe, false excitement.

And now another man had created curls of excitement. A man as unlike Jason Norwich as water was unlike wine. The single comparison between J.B. and

Jason was that both of them were men, as wine and water were both liquid.

Lying tense and shivery in her bed, Nicole's overtired imagination followed and enlarged upon the thread of her own comparison.

Jason, of course, was, or had been, the heady stuff of sparkling wine, effervescent, intoxicating, bubbly at the beginning but quickly losing its sparkle.

J.B., on the other hand, was the more common stuff of water, at times serene, at others turbulent, seemingly tasteless and bland yet with the power to transform a desert into a blossoming Eden, dependable and life sustaining.

And Nicole had recently acquired a raging thirst.

What was he like as a lover?

Closing her eyes, Nicole groaned aloud at the question posed by her teasing imagination. And yet the speculation lured her. Would J.B. be gentle or demanding with a woman? Would he be silent or whispery vocal when aroused? Would he be smooth or endearingly uncertain or, perhaps, an enticing combination of both? Would he kiss a woman until she longed to dissolve into him?

Suddenly warm, Nicole tossed the top sheet aside and forced herself to breathe slowly, deeply. What did she think she was doing? she asked herself scathingly. She had set eyes on the man less than twenty-four hours ago! And already she was getting all hot and bothered by speculating what kind of a lover he was! Had she spent four years of her life finding her soul only to turn around and immediately lose her mind?

Josh Barnet was only a man, for heaven's sake!

Sighing, Nicole shifted onto her side and settled down to sleep. Her very last coherent thought was: *I want his mouth.*

Four

In a small one-story house within walking distance of the main ranch house, J.B. courted sleep without much hope of winning its hand.

Grunting his self-disgust, J.B. levered his tired body up, propping himself on his good arm to peer at the round face of the alarm clock set on the bedside table. A low groan vibrated in his throat as he registered the time. A little more than two hours remained before the alarm would sound its shrill summons.

Easing down onto his back, J.B. flung one arm over his eyes and willed his mind to sleep. His mind had other ideas—all of them concerning the disruptive arrival of his boss's guest.

Damn! How was it possible for one human being to be so beautiful? he mused, yawning widely. Even with the scar that marred one cheek, Nicole Vanzant was the most beautiful woman he'd ever seen. That he'd reacted to her beauty was understandable, though a bit uncomfortable. And J.B. was confident of his ability to cope with his own physical demands; there were ways to assuage the hunger of the flesh. But the hunger of the soul? That was an altogether different reaction.

And now, at two-thirty on a workday morning, J.B.'s soul cried out with starvation.

If only he hadn't awakened exactly when he did in the nursery, he thought, shifting restlessly. Five or ten minutes either way and he wouldn't have overheard the question Barbara had asked Nicole. The query had rooted him, however unwilling, to the floor in the double doorway to the living room.

"You loved Jason very much?"

But J.B. had heard Barbara's question, and he had subsequently heard Nicole's response and the honesty with which she'd answered. J.B.'s reaction to her honesty came straight from his soul—and that was not as easily dealt with as the physical discomfort.

Nicole had loved, too quickly and unwisely, and she had paid the price for her impetuousness, physically and emotionally. Her very acceptance of the enormity of the cost pierced J.B. to the depths of his being.

J.B. had wanted Nicole in the physical sense from the instant he'd seen her. He still wanted her, only now the longing had become complicated by a yearning from a deeper source. The complication denied him escape into slumber.

By the time Nicole awoke, the sun was high and J.B. had already put in over six hours of hard work. Her energy restored by deep, dreamless sleep, Nicole stretched luxuriously, then sprang from bed. She was hungry, and after glancing at the bedside clock, she whipped her nightgown over her head, then headed for the bathroom. She'd missed breakfast by several hours, and if she didn't get a move on, she'd miss lunch, as well.

Fifteen minutes later, dressed in a tailored, men's-style cotton shirt in a hot coral color, hip-hugging designer jeans and low-heeled ankle boots, Nicole breezed into the kitchen.

"Good morning," she caroled cheerfully. "Or should I say good afternoon?"

"Whichever," Ellie responded, a smile lending youthfulness to her weathered face. "As long as it's good." Still smiling, she turned back to the salad she was tossing in a wooden bowl.

"And it obviously is from the bright-eyed look of you," Barbara chimed in, pausing in the act of setting the table to glance at Nicole's tall, elegant form. "Gosh, you look fantastic in jeans," she complimented sincerely.

"Thank you." Skirting the table, Nicole impulsively threw her arm around her friend to give her a brief hug. "And I do feel good." She laughed softly. "In fact, I feel great!"

"But hungry?" Ellie guessed accurately.

"Famished," Nicole answered, grinning happily.

"Well, we're having salad." Ellie slanted a dry glance at Barbara. "We're starting a diet this morning—" she paused "—again. But you can have anything you like—" she paused again "—as long as what you'd like is something we've got."

A devilish gleam lit Nicole's eyes. "I think I'd like to start with a mimosa," she said, licking her lips as if already savoring the taste of the champagne and orange juice cocktail.

"We've got that," Ellie said blandly. "Barbara, go raid Thack's wine supply for a bottle of Dom—"

"Hey!" Nicole laughed. "I was only kidding!"

"That's good," Ellie retorted. "Thack would likely spit a curse if we opened his last bottle for breakfast."

"Especially since he's not here to get his share," Barbara inserted wryly. Walking to the refrigerator, she continued, "How about something less exotic, like steak and eggs?"

"Steak?" Nicole repeated, frowning. "For breakfast?"

"You're in Texas, honey," Ellie drawled thickly. "Steak and eggs is a tradition in Texas . . . at least for ranchin' Texans."

The devilish gleam jumped back into Nicole's eyes. "Did she say ranchin' or raunchy?" she asked Barbara innocently.

Barbara pretended to consider the question. "I think she said ranchin'," she finally decided. "But from my own personal experience with one particular rancher, I suspect the two might be synonymous."

"That's for damn sure," Ellie snorted. "And we womenfolk wouldn't want 'em any other way."

"Too true," Barbara agreed, then gazed at Nicole. "Steak?"

Nicole narrowed her eyes. "Did you eat steak for breakfast?"

"Of course," Barbara said blithely. "Four ounces, broiled. I'm on a diet, remember?"

"I can't imagine why," Nicole retorted, skimming an expert gaze the length of Barbara's softly rounded body. "I think you look terrific the way you are."

"Told ya," Ellie muttered, vigorously tossing the salad vegetables.

"I'll tell you why," Barbara said fiercely. "I can't get into most of my clothes." She planted her hands on her hips. "Last chance, Nicki," she warned. "If you want me to cook breakfast for you, say so now or forever hold your peace."

Startled by her friend's sudden outburst, Nicole gaped at her, then sputtered, "I . . . I . . . Barbara, I'll cook my own breakfast!"

"Oh, for gosh field's sake!" Ellie exploded, swinging away from the counter to plunk the salad bowl on the table. "Barbara Holcomb Sharp! You oughta be ashamed of yourself!" She turned to Nicole. "Young lady, you just sit down. *I'll* cook breakfast for you." She tilted her head to fix a stern glance on her niece. "And you come over here and eat your lunch. Your stomach's likely as empty as your head." Stomping to the refrigerator, she brushed Barbara aside, then began pulling food from the large unit.

Her cheeks flushed, Barbara crossed the room to sit down opposite Nicole. "I'm sorry I was rude," she said in a controlled tone. "But I'm getting a little touchy about my weight."

Reaching across the table, Nicole grasped Barbara's hand. "But it has only been two weeks since Rita was born. I think you look wonderful. I can't believe you're this upset over ten pounds."

"It's really twenty," Barbara muttered.

"Okay, twenty." Nicole shrugged. "What's the big deal?"

"I'll tell you what the big deal is," Ellie said impatiently, turning away from the steak sizzling on the stove-top grill. "She's afraid that if she don't get back to modeling weight, her man might develop a roving eye."

Stunned, Nicole stared at Barbara in wide-eyed astonishment. In her opinion, the additional weight gave Barbara a voluptuous allure she'd never possessed while modeling. "I don't believe—"

"I will not allow myself to become fat and unattractive!" Barbara cut in on Nicole in a wail. "Thack fell in love with a slender model. He teased me about my roundness while I was pregnant." She glared defiantly at her aunt. "Yes, I'm going to make sure Thack has no reason to look elsewhere—even if I have to starve myself!"

Sighing, Ellie turned back to the stove. She put the steak on a warm plate and switched off the grill. When she set the plate before Nicole, Ellie noticed the suspicious brightness in Barbara's eyes. Sighing again, she sat down next to her niece.

"Ah, honey, do you realize how unfair you're being to Thack?" she asked.

"Unfair! By wanting to keep myself attractive for him?" Barbara protested.

"That man loves you, honey." Ellie's voice was firm with solid conviction. "*You*, the woman you are, not just the packaging." A chiding smile curved her pale lips. "You forget, I knew Thack a spell before you met him, and I'm telling you he's a different man today. He's content. And if he teases you, it's a loving teasing because that man purely loves to tease you. *You*, his woman, not some nervous, underfed, high-strung New York model."

Lowering her gaze to the table, Barbara whispered, "I know, but still . . ."

"Barbara!" Ellie snapped. "Can you honestly tell me the scars on Thackery's back make him less attractive to you?"

"Of course not!" Barbara jerked her head up to confront her aunt. "But that's not the same thing!"

What scars? Nicole wondered, switching her gaze from Barbara to Ellie.

"It's exactly the same thing," Ellie retorted. "Packaging. So, okay, maybe Thack was attracted by the package at the beginning. But then so were you. And he was all gold, and handsome, and you couldn't see the scars, not on his back and not on his leg, and not the ones inside. But when you did get to see them, all of them, did they turn you off?"

Two tears slipped over Barbara's lids to roll unnoticed down her face. "No," she said steadily.

Ellie's stern expression gentled, as did her voice. "Course not. And your rounded bottom's not gonna turn Thack off, either," the older woman said with the wisdom of sixty-odd years of living. "Honey, it's a good thing to want to look your best for your man, but not if you drive yourself and everyone else crazy while you're doing it."

Barbara bit her lip, then she nodded and smiled. "You're right, Aunt Ellie." Leaning over, she kissed her aunt's leathery cheek, murmuring, "As usual. Thank you. I'll clean up my act, I promise." Barbara glanced at Nicole as she straightened. "I'm sorry."

"What for?" Nicole managed to ask from a tight throat.

"For snapping at you on your first morning here," Barbara replied, then smiled. "And for behaving like a paranoid ditz."

"You're neither paranoid nor a ditz." Nicole denied Barbara's assertion while accepting that the description fit her own behavior more accurately—*she* had been behaving like a paranoid ditz for four years! "You're a warm, caring woman," Nicole continued, smiling softly, "who just happens to be very much in love with her husband."

"That's right," Ellie said with a suspicious roughness. "So eat your salad and stop worrying." She slanted her sharp-eyed gaze at Nicole. "And you eat your steak before it's stone-cold."

The tension eased, the meal was consumed in a congenial atmosphere, but the conversation would haunt Nicole for a long time afterward.

While the women ate a leisurely lunch in the comfortably cool kitchen, J.B. and Thack sat hunched in the meager shade provided by a dust-coated pickup truck. They were eating sandwiches containing thick slices of roast beef, washed down by deep swallows of beer.

"So what do you think of our guest?" Thack unwittingly initiated the subject burning a hole in J.B.'s mind.

"Pretty," J.B. said, concentrating on the toe of one scuffed boot.

"Pretty, hell!" Thack retorted. "Nicole is stunning."

Recalling the bemused expression on Thack's face the night before, J.B.'s thin lips flattened.

"You beginning to feel itchy, Thack?" he asked evenly.

Thack shot J.B. a frowning look. "Itchy? What are you talking about?"

"Being hobbled to one woman," J.B. answered, meeting Thack's eyes head-on. "I couldn't help but see your expression last night in Rita's room when Nicole kissed you. You looked fascinated and interested, and as you said, Nicole is one stunning woman." Though it didn't show by as much as a flicker on his face, J.B. felt his muscles tauten when Thack grinned.

"I'm interested in Nicole," the tall man admitted freely, "but not in the way you mean." Thack shook his blond head. "No, ol' son, I'm sure as hell not getting itchy in that way. That feisty ex-model is enough woman for me. I'd die for Barbara," Thack vowed with quiet simplicity. Then he frowned again. "I thought you knew that."

"I thought so, too, but..." As J.B.'s voice trailed away, Thack's grew stronger.

"There are no buts." Thack got up, his brown eyes glittering dangerously. "I'll say this just one time, friend, so listen up. I'm only interested in Nicole because she is Barbara's friend, and I know something of her story." He glared at J.B. "Got that?"

"Yeah." Looking anything but intimidated, J.B. grinned at his boss. "While you're up there, you can get me another beer." He was quiet until Thack had pulled two cans from the cooler and was hunkered down again in the sketchy shade. "So what is Nicole's story?" J.B. asked in a deceptively unconcerned tone as he popped the top on the can.

Thack wasn't deceived. Arching his eyebrows, he gave J.B. a droll look. "I can't help but wonder which one of us is more interested in Nicole," he observed dryly. "And for what reasons."

"Okay, I'm interested," J.B. admitted easily. "For all the obvious reasons," he continued after taking a deep swallow of the cold beer. "So what's her story?" he repeated pointedly.

"I don't know all of it," Thack said, digging another sandwich from the insulated bag. "You want another?" Hand still in the bag, he glanced up at J.B., who nodded. "Ham and cheese or another roast beef?" Thack inquired, frowning at the sandwiches he held in one hand.

"Whatever," J.B. drawled. "Will you get on with it?" he asked politely, fully aware that Thack was baiting him.

"You're really interested in this woman, huh?" Thack persisted, handing over one of the sandwiches.

Sighing loudly, J.B. accepted the sandwich, removed the plastic it was wrapped in and bit into it before responding to Thack's obvious ploy for information. Chewing slowly, J.B. considered exactly how much he should reveal to his employer and best friend. "I was hard-pressed not to grab her and take her with me to my place last night," he finally replied. "That answer your question?"

"No." Thack shook his head. "All that tells me is that you want to take her to bed."

"So?" J.B. challenged softly.

Thack's smile spoke of years of friendship. "I think it's a mite more involved than that. Come on, buddy," he chided. "Let's get it out in the open and examine it."

J.B.'s lips curved into a sardonic smile. "I might be willing to do that—if I understood it myself. Nicole affects me in a way I can't explain, even to myself." His shoulders moved in a half shrug. "That's why I was trying to pump you for information about her."

Thack's eyes narrowed, and he frowned as he thought. "Well, let me see if I can remember exactly what Barbara told me." Shifting, he made himself as comfortable as possible. J.B. watched and waited with hard-won patience.

"As I recall, Barbara told me that before the accident Nicole was the most beautiful woman she had ever seen, and working in the modeling business, she had seen many beautiful women."

"Including herself," J.B. murmured.

Thack's eyes glowed softly. "Yeah. At the time I couldn't imagine a woman more beautiful than Barb." He shook his head as if still not certain his eyes had not deceived him. "But when I got a look at Nicole yesterday, I understood what Barb meant. Hell, even with the scar Nicole is stunning."

"Yeah." A wealth of emotions were woven through the word that sighed through J.B.'s lips.

"Anyway," Thack went on, slanting a thoughtful glance at J.B., "apparently Nicole was at the height of success when she got involved with the wrong crowd."

"Not the wrong crowd," J.B. corrected. "The wrong man."

Thack made a sour face. "If you know this story, why bug me to tell it? We're wasting time here, you know."

"No, we're not," J.B. said flatly. "And I wanted to compare what I know to what you know. So get on with it."

"I don't know too much more to go on with,"
Thack growled. "All Barb said was that Nicole seemed
to get caught up in partying all the time, keeping late
hours—that sort of thing. She and two men were in a
small sports car, driving back to Manhattan from a
party on Long Island. Barb said the man driving was
high. He ran head-on into a sixteen wheeler. He and
the other man were killed instantly. Nicole had fallen
asleep on the back seat. It saved her life, even though
she was seriously injured. Barbara believes Nicole was
in love with the man who was driving."

"Wrong," J.B. said tonelessly.

"Dammit, J.B.!" Thack barked. "How do you
know that?"

J.B. lifted one shoulder. "I overheard Barbara and
Nicole talking last night as I was on my way out."

"You overheard?" Thack asked mockingly. "You
were indulging in a bit of eavesdropping?"

Crossing his legs Indian-style, J.B. rose smoothly to
his feet. Gazing down at Thack, he taunted, "I
couldn't help myself. I was fascinated and interested." As he turned away, he chided, "Time to get
back to work...boss."

"Wait a damned minute, Barnet!" Thack grumbled, springing up to stride after the other man.
"What precisely are your intentions? Nicole's a guest
in my house, you know."

Coming to an abrupt halt, J.B. whipped around.
His eyes were bright with amusement. A rakish grin
tugged at his lips. "My intentions?" he repeated on a
burst of laughter. "Are you kidding?"

Thack wasn't laughing. "No, J.B., I'm dead serious."

"So am I, Thack," J.B. shot back solemnly. "I intend having her—all of her."

Staring steadily at J.B., Thack drew himself up to his full six feet four inches. "Nicole's vulnerable, Josh. And I won't stand by and watch her be hurt while she's on my land." Cold conviction laced Thack's soft tone.

His stance easy, J.B. stared impassively at Thack. "I have never deliberately hurt a woman in my life," he said softly. "And you know it."

"That's right," Thack admitted. "But this woman's different. She has only recently come out of hiding. As I said, she's extremely vulnerable." His mouth twisted wryly. "I somehow doubt she's a match for you."

"Then again you might just be selling her short," J.B. retorted. "We'll see."

"As you can obviously see, the house is much too small for a family," Barbara said, indicating the single-level dwelling. "Even though Thack's great-grandfather raised a family in it," she modified with a laugh. "And Thack's grandfather lived in it with his wife and three children while he was building the house we live in."

"It appears to be in excellent repair," Nicole observed, noting the fresh coat of white paint on the house and the neatly kept yard with a picket fence around it.

"Hmmm." Barbara nodded. "It's been home for a lot of ranch foremen since Thack's grandfather moved his family into the big house."

They were standing under the wide-spreading branches of an old oak tree a few feet from the gleaming white fence. It was midafternoon, and the sun was merciless. Squinting against the glare of sunlight beyond the delicious patch of dark shade, Nicole stared at the house and tried to imagine what the inside looked like. If a home reflected the resident's personality, perhaps the interior would give her a clue to what went on inside Josh Barnet's mind.

"And now J.B. lives in it," she murmured.

"Temporarily, anyway," Barbara said softly.

"Temporarily?" Nicole repeated, startled by the sense of apprehension that rippled through her. "What do you mean? Is J.B. quitting his job?" Half turning, she studied Barbara's face.

"No." Barbara shook her head, then shrugged. "At least not yet. He seems content here, but..." Her voice faded into a sigh.

"But?" Nicole prompted, needing to know, but not even sure why.

Raising a hand, Barbara tugged her sleeveless blouse away from her chest. "J.B. is an excellent rancher," she finally answered. "He was born and raised on a ranch up near Fort Worth. He knows the land, and he knows the stock. But his first love is police work." Barbara slid her hand around her neck to lift her hair away from her skin. "Thack's positive that J.B. will go back to the force someday."

"But can he?" Nicole frowned. "I mean, with the..." She let her voice trail away as if unable to speak of his handicap.

"Artificial limb," Barbara finished for her. "Oh, yes, he can. He was offered a promotion and a desk job after the accident. He turned both down."

"I don't understand," Nicole said slowly. "If he loves the work, why turn it down?"

Barbara's smile was sad. "Thack believes that J.B. thought the offer was just a gesture at the time, a thank-you measure for giving his arm in the line of duty."

"Does Thack believe it, too?"

"Not Thack." Barbara smiled. "Thack claims that J.B. was the best man on the Fort Worth force. He maintains that the promotion was overdue. But what J.B. forgot was that even with losing his arm, he got the man he was chasing. The state won a conviction of drug trafficking against the man, too."

Drugs. Nicole felt a chill. She would carry scars for the rest of her life because one man was using drugs. And J.B. had lost a part of himself because another man was smuggling drugs. Nicole wanted to scream her fury at the stupidity of it all. But she didn't scream; she sighed.

"Oh, Lord, I think I'm melting!" Barbara moaned. "Let's go back inside where it's cool."

As they walked back to the main house, Nicole glanced over the property. There were several buildings besides the large ranch house and the small foreman's residence, and every one of them was in pristine condition. Even to an untrained eye it was obvious that Thack loved and took pride in his heritage.

After mounting the steps to the spacious porch, Nicole turned to gaze into the distance, through the heat waves radiating from the rolling, rocky hills. With very little imagination she could picture a line of small, rugged horsemen strung out along a ridge.

Caught up in the mythos of the land and its inhabitants, Nicole merely nodded when Barbara said she was going inside. No longer aware of the stifling heat, or even the heavy feel of her tight jeans, she stared in fascination at the vast terrain spread out before her and recalled what she had read of its history.

This country was the fabled stomping ground of the savage nomads who had migrated south from the Rockies. This chunk of Texas was part of the sweeping Great Plains, the domain of the peoples who had taken to the horse as a fledgling takes to the sky. This was the territory ruled by the fearsome tribes known as the Comanche.

And J.B. was out there somewhere on the land.

The jolt of alarm that speared through Nicole at first startled her, then brought a shaky, uncertain smile to her lips. The Comanche were long gone, but even in the present there were dangers out there on the land. A man had to remain alert to his surroundings to remain alive.

Of course, both J.B. and Thack had lived the majority of their lives on the cutting edge of danger.

Turning to enter the house, Nicole took comfort from the thought until another thought struck her. At one crucial point J.B. had slipped off that edge; the fall had severed the lower part of his left arm. Nicole shivered moments before she stepped inside the air-conditioned coolness of the house.

Five

"Nicki would like to see the inside of your house, J.B."
Barbara offered him the information over the dinner
table, along with a serving dish of steaming vegetables.

Nicole was suddenly overwhelmed by an urge to
crawl under the oval oak table. The urge grew as J.B.
slanted a contemplative glance at her.

"Really?" he asked softly. "Why?"

Her face growing warm, Nicole shifted uneasily on
her chair. "I, er, it's very old, isn't it?" she responded unevenly. "I was just curious, that's all."
Glancing away from his steady regard, Nicole cringed
inside as she caught sight of the bright smile on Barbara's face and wondered why Thack was scowling.
"It really isn't necessary," she added hurriedly.

J.B.'s expression didn't alter by as much as a twitch.
"I'll show you the inside of the house," he said in the

same soft tone, "but Thack could tell you more about its history. It *is* his house."

Feeling oddly breathless, Nicole turned to look at Thack, a part of her hoping he'd offer to be her guide, another part praying he wouldn't. Barbara settled the issue before Thack had a chance to speak.

"Thack may own the house," she said reasonably, "but you live in it, J.B. And you know as much of its history as he does. You must," she added dryly, "you've heard it often enough."

"Barbara." There was a hint of warning underlying Thack's tone that Nicole didn't understand. But apparently she did.

"Thackery," she returned sweetly, "stay out of this."

This time there was a twitch in J.B.'s expression, right at the corners of his mouth. "We can walk over to the house as soon as we've finished dinner, if you like."

Alone? In the dark? Nicole tried to deny the charge of excitement that crackled through her body at the thought of being alone with the intimidating man. What in the world would they talk about? she wondered, stealing a quick glance at his mouth. If they were alone, completely alone, *would* they talk? The speculation activated her mind and her mouth.

"Uh, I, ah, had promised to give Rita her bath after dinner!" Feeling like an absolute idiot, Nicole gazed beseechingly at Barbara.

Barbara merely smiled.

Thack continued to scowl.

Aunt Ellie looked confused.

"I'll wait." J.B.'s tone was adamant.

Nicole gave up. Pulling her fragmented composure and senses together, she smiled coolly. "All right," she agreed. She knew she should add a thank-you, but she simply couldn't get it out. Avoiding his eyes, Nicole applied herself to the delicious meal she tasted not at all.

Bathing the tiny infant proved a special delight for Nicole, and was accomplished much too soon. Laughing every time a flailing, slippery arm or leg escaped her gentle grasp, Nicole forgot her initial fear of handling the child and thoroughly enjoyed every minute of the ritual. When Rita was clean, powdered and ready for her bottle, Nicole reluctantly relinquished the baby into the waiting arms of her father.

"Hi, beautiful," Thack said conversationally to his wide-eyed, solemn daughter as he cradled her against his chest. "I missed not seeing you all day. Did you miss me?"

Smiling mistily, Nicole softly shut the door, closing father and daughter together in a moment of their own, far away from the harsh realities of the world.

Reality caught up with Nicole when she heard the attractive sound of J.B.'s quiet voice as she descended the stairs. Pausing in the foyer, she smoothed her palms over her shoulder-length dark hair, then down the silky material of the skirt covering her slim hips. J.B. laughed softly and caused a riot of crazy reactions in her body. For one long second Nicole was tempted to dash back up the stairs and hide out until J.B. realized she wasn't going with him and went back to his house alone. Then, lifting her head, she squashed the urge. She was done with dashing away and hiding. With a cool smile that she hoped concealed her conflicting emotions, Nicole sauntered into the living room.

"Ready?" In one fluid movement J.B. was on his feet and crossing the floor to her.

"Yes, I . . ." Nicole swallowed the words "suppose so" and repeated, "Yes."

"It's a lovely night for a stroll," Barbara observed brightly, making a shooing motion at Nicole behind J.B.'s back. "Enjoy yourselves. I won't wait up." Her hazel eyes gleamed with mischief as she watched the color climb into Nicole's cheeks.

"Barbara, honestly." Nicole sighed in exasperation.

"Glad to hear it," J.B. murmured, curling the fingers of his right hand around her arm to escort her to the front door. "Good night, Barbara."

It was a lovely night. After the intense heat of the afternoon, the fresh, cool zephyr playing through the trees and over the land felt like a soothing balm to a stinging sunburn. The gentle breeze carried the scent of the earth. Inhaling deeply, Nicole stepped from the porch and gazed up at the night sky.

"So it's true," she murmured in an awed tone. "The stars do appear bigger and brighter here."

"Like you could reach up and touch them?"

Nicole laughed self-consciously. "Yes," she confessed. "I feel as though I could reach out and gather a handful."

"And do what with them?" J.B. asked very softly, loosening his fingers to slide them the length of her arm.

The skimming brush of his fingers was like a tongue of fire licking her skin. "I...I don't know. Bring them out to look at on a bleak day, I suppose." When his

hand slid against her palm and his fingers laced with
hers, Nicole couldn't control a shiver of response; she
had a hard enough time of it controlling her breathing!

"By then they'd be dead and cold." Tugging gently,
he began walking toward the small house. "A bleak
day calls for life and fire."

"Such as?" Nicole challenged tautly, moving beside him automatically, but not looking at him.

"A warm drink," J.B. suggested, his voice a caressing whisper. "And a hot man."

"I've known that kind of life and fire," Nicole said
tightly, moving past the gate he held open for her.
"There is little comfort when the drink and the man
are gone."

"Maybe you tasted the wrong brew and the wrong
man." J.B. paused on the shadowy porch, his hand
poised over the old-fashioned latch on the door.

"Maybe," Nicole conceded when it became clear he
wasn't going to move until she responded.

The door was not locked. His chuckle a mere murmur of sound blending with the other natural night
sounds, J.B. pressed the latch and pushed the door
open. Reaching inside, he flicked a switch, bathing the
interior with soft light before moving back for her to
precede him.

There was no foyer or entryway. Crossing the
threshold, Nicole stepped into the small, square living room and was immediately enveloped by a feeling
of warmth that seemed almost as if she'd come home.
Frowning at the odd sensation, she moved into the
center of the room, her gaze slowly roaming over the
interior.

The furnishings were sparse, but Nicole instinctively knew they had not come with the house but had been selected with thought and care by the man standing very close, too close, beside her. Half expecting to see a lot of dark leather, she was pleasantly surprised by the vibrant colors swirling through the smooth material covering a long sofa and two deep, comfortable-looking recliner chairs. In the swirling pattern a rich shade of rust blended into a pumpkin hue that, in turn, merged with spicy cinnabar. Plump velour toss pillows were a splash of buttery yellow in each corner of the sofa. The color scheme was picked up and reflected in the large oval braided rug in the middle of the natural pine floor. There were no objects or knickknacks scattered on the highly polished end tables. Satiny-looking brass lamps were the sole adornment on the tables. The old-parchment shade of the walls carried through the theme of earth tones.

Nicole was instantly delighted by the room, but what surprised and delighted her most of all was the abundance of plant life. Painted clay pots filled with lacy-leafed ferns hung from the exposed beams in the ceiling. More clay pots filled with green leafy plants were banked to one side of the wide stone fireplace. Another grouping of pots containing a variety of cacti overflowed shelves on the other side of the fireplace.

Taking up the entire short wall that Nicole assumed separated the living room from the kitchen were floor-to-ceiling shelves packed tightly with books, both paperback and hardcover. There was a section in the very center of the wall, two shelves deep, in which was set a disk stereo unit. Nicole's fingers itched to examine his reading and listening material.

As she had suspected it would, the room revealed much to Nicole about the man. As J.B. himself, the room had no frills, was not fussy. It was neat, it was cool, but the colors and plants lent warmth and life. The room was honest; it mirrored the man.

"There's more to the house than this one room, you know."

Nicole started, then laughed softly. She had been quiet too long, she knew, but she was completely captivated. "I know," she finally murmured. "But I'd be quite happy to remain right here."

"You like it?" There was nothing at all offhand about J.B.'s tone; he expected an honest answer. Giving him anything less would have been impossible for Nicole.

"I love it." Tilting her head, she met his watchful stare. "Is the house air-conditioned, or is it the ambiance that gives it a cooling effect?"

J.B.'s slow smile chased away the cool feeling by sending fiery streaks through her body. "It's air-conditioned, but I'm glad you approve of the effect."

"Why?" Nicole held her breath; the one-word question was so simple, and so very complex.

"Because we both now know that you are going to be spending a lot of your time here," J.B. answered immediately in a soft but firmly confident tone. "Especially the nights."

Breathing was difficult. Responding to him was impossible. Nicole merely shivered and stared at J.B. She was unsure of what she felt—the uncertainty made her wary; the cloudiness in her eyes revealed her emotions. But she was not afraid.

His smile gentled, softening the unrelenting lines of his face. Lifting his hand, J.B. stroked her hair from her temple to where it rested on her shoulder. "Please don't be afraid of me, Nicole. I promise I won't hurt you." As J.B. murmured the assurance, he twined his fingers into the silky thickness of her dark hair.

Nicole didn't even try to hide her reaction to his touch. "I'm not afraid," she said, swallowing to moisten her dry throat. "But I am unsure," she admitted, gazing into his beautiful eyes. "We've just met. We barely know each other. We—"

"Both know it's right," J.B. murmured, finishing for her. His fingers slid through the strands of her hair, then curled around her nape. "I wanted to be with you, like this, from the moment I saw you hovering uncertainly in the doorway yesterday." The smile on his thin lips faded to a blatantly sensual curve as, applying gentle pressure, he drew her head close to his. "And, deliberate or not, during lunch you made me feel like I was burning alive."

Nicole's breath was reduced to short, uneven puffs. "What . . . what do you mean?"

"You wanted my mouth," J.B. murmured, closing the distance to a whisper between their lips. "Now take what you want."

Nicole obeyed instinctively. Parting her lips, she brushed them tentatively over his. Then, with a low moan of need, she fitted her lips to the contour of his mouth.

J.B.'s response was immediate and devastating. Releasing her nape, his fingers speared into her hair, his palm cupping the back of her head to hold her steady while his mouth fused with hers. His tongue didn't hesitate to tentatively test the waters but boldly thrust into the sweet depths of her mouth. His stroking, searching tongue ignited a blaze in Nicole that burned out of control and raced wildly through her body.

Reacting to the immediacy of a need unlike anything she had ever experienced before, Nicole's mouth clung to his while her tongue teased his into an erotic duel.

The kiss ended as quickly as it had begun. Nicole had barely enough time to begin to feel disoriented when J.B. abruptly pulled away from her. Releasing her hair, he grasped her hand, then pivoting, he strode toward a narrow door, taking her with him. Flinging the door open, he led her straight into the center of his bedroom.

Even with her senses reeling Nicole wanted to examine the room J.B. slept in. Fascinated, barely aware that he had released his grasp on her hand, she glanced around slowly, her avid gaze missing nothing.

J.B.'s bedroom was a veritable bower of plant life. In clay pots large and small, hanging from the ceiling, banked under the two long narrow windows and sitting on the floor, the room was vibrant with life, growing life. The walls were painted forest green, the woodwork sparkling white. As in the living room, the furniture was sparse, constructed of natural wood, with clean lines and a rich, polished patina. The focal point of the room was the bed—it was round and enormous.

In her bemusement with what the room was telling her about the man, Nicole thought she heard a muted thud. She ignored it. A tingle of anticipation tiptoeing down her spine, she stared at his bed. The second soft thud sent icy hot shards of excitement throughout her body; Nicole had identified what had caused the thudding sound. She really didn't have to turn to look, but she did just the same.

His narrow feet bare, J.B. was standing by the double dresser, methodically emptying the contents of his jeans pockets and dropping the items on the dresser top. Scattered around him on the floor were his dark socks and gleaming dress boots. As she watched, his ungloved hand moved to the buckle on the leather belt around his lean waist. The act of unfastening the buckle unlocked her frozen tongue.

"Aren't you being a bit, er, presumptuous?" she asked in a voice that sounded crackly in the silent room.

"You tell me," J.B. responded softly, unhesitatingly flipping the snap on the waistband of his jeans. "Am I being a bit, er, presumptuous?"

Nicole felt the glide of the jean zipper as acutely as if it ran the length of her spine. "I..." Her mouth went dry as he slid the denim down and over his muscular thighs.

"Yes?" A hint of a smile teased his lips as he simultaneously kicked off the jeans and glanced up at her.

A silent groan tore at Nicole's parched throat. Clad in nothing but a shirt and very, very brief briefs, J.B. presented an intimidating picture of sheer masculinity.

His masculinity called out blatantly to everything feminine in Nicole. She was hot. She was cold. She was ready. And yet, after four years of abstinence and self-recrimination, she was wary.

"I didn't say I'd go to bed with you," she said in a choked whisper.

The smile on J.B.'s lips took on a chiding slant. His movements slow, controlled, he walked over to her. "That's right, you didn't say you'd go to bed with me." As he came to a halt mere inches from her, his hand lifted to the buttons of her blouse. "But then you didn't have to say it," as he murmured to her the buttons fell open, "did you?"

Nicole's throat was dry, her stomach felt hollow, her thighs were trembling. She wanted this man, wanted him in the most intimate manner. She knew it. He knew it, too. She shook her head as he slowly slid the blouse off her shoulders and down her arms.

"No." Nicole's voice was a breathy sigh. "It didn't have to be said." Without thought or hesitation she stepped out of the skirt he sent slithering down her legs. She stepped out of her sandals at the same time. Her heart thumped painfully when he moved back to sweep a blazing blue gaze over her scantily clad body.

"A teddy." J.B.'s tone was low, throaty. "A red teddy."

Unable to decipher his tone, Nicole felt suddenly exposed and unsure and had to fight an urge to cross her arms over her breasts. Her only undergarment was a teddy. It was flame red and predominantly lace.

"You..." Nicole had to pause to wet her lips. "You have an aversion to teddies?" she finally managed to ask.

"Aversion?" For an instant J.B. looked as if he might laugh. He didn't, but his smile was sex personified. "Oh, Nicki, you'll never know." Moving slowly, he backed her to the end of the bed.

He was close, so close. Nicole could feel the heat of his body, could smell the combined scent of musky after-shave and musky man, could see the fire of desire dancing in the sapphire depths of his eyes. She wanted nothing more than to excite, entice, pleasure this man. She trembled with the longing to be pleasured in turn.

"I've fantasized about you, in a teddy, stretched out across my bed." Other than his warm breath caressing her parted lips, J.B. didn't touch her. The black-gloved hand moved, no more than a twitching wave. "Will you indulge my fantasy?"

Intensified to a quivering mass of willingness, Nicole held J.B.'s gaze and slowly moved onto the bed. When he swallowed, she swallowed. When he trembled, she trembled. When he groaned, she smiled and slowly, sensuously stretched her long, elegant body out for his visual pleasure.

"You move like a woman inviting a lover." J.B.'s beautiful voice was reduced to a hoarse murmur.

"Yesss." Drawing the word out on a hissing whisper, Nicole curled her arms up and over her head, slid the tip of her tongue over her lips and parted her long legs with restless abandon.

J.B. needed no further enticement. With a controlled sweep of his hand, his briefs were whisked from his body. Then he was moving onto the bed. Poised over her, he lowered his mouth to hers.

J.B.'s kiss was pure, unadulterated ravishment. Nicole reveled in it. Her lips clinging to his, her tongue darting into his mouth, she undulated beneath him, gliding her silk-clad body against his. J.B. groaned his pleasure; Nicole frowned at being denied the feel of his skin.

As he slid his mouth from hers, she slid her arms down, between them. As his tongue traced the faint but sensitive scar on her cheek, her trembling fingers undid the buttons on his shirt. As her hands spread over the warmth of his lightly haired chest, he thrust his hips into hers.

"Feel me, Nicole," he growled softly into her ear. "I can't wait much longer. I must be with you, inside you, part of you." She could feel the tremor in the fingers that tugged the teddy from her flushed body.

"Yes, please!" Her nakedness giving her a sense of freedom and power, Nicole arched her body against his while her hands smoothed the shirt from his shoulders.

"No!"

Stunned by the sound of pain in his harsh command, the gliding motion of her hands ceased abruptly. Her body instinctively pressing back, away from him, Nicole's shocked gaze tangled with his.

"Easy, love," J.B. murmured, his lips brushing hers. "I didn't mean to frighten you." He captured her bottom lip and gently pulled it between his, into his mouth. When he felt the tension ease out of her and heard her breathing grow uneven, he pulled back far enough to stare into her smoky eyes. "The shirt stays on." His voice was low and soft but rigid with conviction.

Reason pierced the sensual haze clouding Nicole's mind. A sharp pain of compassion seared her chest at the realization that he did not want her to see the device that gave the world the impression that he was a *whole* man. Nicole knew that the artificial hand and forearm were in some way harnessed to his upper arm and shoulder. By inching her fingertips along his shoulder, she could feel the edge of that harness. Even as her fingers brushed the edge, a low warning growl vibrated in his throat. Out of pride or fear of rejection or something, J.B. refused to allow her to see the contraption.

"Josh." All the understanding and pain she was feeling for him shone out of the tear-filled eyes she raised to his. "Please, let me take off your shirt."

J.B. was shaking his head before she had finished making her plea. "No. The shirt stays on," he repeated flatly. "You can touch me anywhere." His lips curved in a peculiarly sexy way. "I wish you would." The smile disappeared. "But don't touch the harness."

As if burned, Nicole pulled her fingers away from the edge of the strap. "You're being unfair," she protested, absently stroking his warm chest. "Unless I take to the veil, my scar is exposed to the world." As she gently chastised him, the pad of one finger contacted one flat male nipple. A thrill shot through her when he drew in his breath.

J.B.'s eyes darkened to navy as he slowly slid down along her body. "If you take to the veil," he muttered into the curve of her neck, "I'll kiss your scar through it." She felt his lips tilt into a smile. "The prospect is excitingly erotic. Remind me to buy a piece of chiffon next time I go to town." As he spoke, his breath moistened her skin, his lips left a trail of fire to the peak of one breast.

The fire exploded inside Nicole as his lips captured the hardening peak. Electrified, she curled her fingers into the soft, suede-like material of his shirt. The smooth material caressed her palms, sending tingles up her arms to tighten nerve endings at her nape. Torn between the desire to explore the new and exciting sensations created by the friction of fabric against her skin and the need to caress his chest, Nicole clung to the material with the last two fingers of each hand and spread the remaining portion of her hands over his rapidly heating skin.

J.B. showed his appreciation and approval of her actions by sucking gently on her breast and rubbing his hair-rough thighs against the silkiness of hers.

Nicole cried out sharply with pleasure and reacted to it without conscious direction. Digging her fingers into both his shirt and skin, she arched her back and lifted her hips, straining, her empty, hungry body bowed in a silent plea for fulfillment.

"Nicki. Nicole." Her name was a whisper, a prayer on J.B.'s lips as he transferred them from her breast to her mouth. "We will be good together," he promised, entering her slowly. "No," he murmured into her mouth as they became one, "we will be spectacular together."

Tension tightened and coiled deliciously inside Nicole as J.B. moved his hips in a rhythm that was ageless yet ever new. Into her mouth he whispered words shockingly exciting and sensually inflaming. Tension steadily building inside, Nicole dragged her hands down the edges of his shirt to the tailored ends, then still clutching the material, she gripped his hips to urge him deeper and yet deeper inside her.

Release came in a shuddering rush, quaking through Nicole with such force she clasped his hips spasmodically with her thighs and cried his name aloud. An instant later Nicole felt the throb of J.B.'s life-giving ecstasy and heard her name on his strangled gasp.

For one all-encompassing, encapsulated moment every cell, every molecule, every particle that was the sum of J.B. was hers, as every ounce of Nicole's being was his. The height was stunning, breathtaking, but could not be maintained. Normalcy returned with a sigh of uneven breath and the beat of two hearts.

"It was spectacular." Inhaling deeply, J.B. eased his body from hers.

"Yes." A smile teased her lips as she allowed him to gather her body close to his. "Even with the shirt on," she added, burying her laughter against his moist skin.

"Think you could get into kinky sex, hmmm?" J.B.'s chuckle tickled her ear and funny bone.

"What did you have in mind, cowboy?" She laughed, raising her head to give him an arch look.

"We could try leaving the teddy on next time, just undo the little snaps that hold the ends together." His smile was bone melting. "I do like that teddy."

Nicole's laughter faded, and she caught her bottom lip between her teeth for an instant. "If I leave the teddy on next time," she began hesitantly, then finished quickly, "will you take the shirt off?"

J.B. became rigid, his embrace crushing the breath out of her. Then, obviously exerting control, he slowly relaxed. "Not next time, love," he said carefully. "But someday—maybe."

Nicole lowered her eyes to hide a surge of tears. "When you feel you can trust me, you mean?" she asked tightly.

"No." Catching her chin between his thumb and forefinger, J.B. gently lifted her face. "When I feel I can trust me."

"But..."

"Not to fall apart inside," he continued as if she hadn't spoken, "if you have to glance away from the sight of it."

"J.B., I wouldn't!" Nicole protested. Her head dropping, she rubbed her cheek against his chest. "I never would," she murmured, stroking her tongue over his salty skin.

"Are you trying to start something all over again?" Amusement could be heard in his velvet-rough voice. The obvious reaction of his body told her he wasn't merely trying to change the subject.

"Could I?" she asked innocently but hopefully.

"Do you want to put the teddy on?" he shot back innocently but hopefully.

Laughing delightedly, Nicole flung herself onto her back. "To hell with the teddy—" she laughed, tugging him over her "—and the shirt! Kiss me, cowboy." Clasping his face with her hands, she drew his mouth to hers.

This time their lovemaking was wildly free and exhilarating and over much too soon. Exhausted, they lay side by side, just smiling at one another.

"Spectacular again?" Nicole asked around a grin.

"Mind-blowing," J.B. replied solemnly. "I think my brain's been scrambled."

"Umm, yes." Nicole nodded. "That's one way of putting it."

Laughing softly, J.B. rolled onto his side, propping his head on his hand to gaze into her flushed face. "This could become habit-forming, you know."

Sobering, Nicole blinked up at him. "I know."

"It bothers you?" J.B. asked sharply.

Nicole moved her head restlessly against the rumpled sheet; the pillow had fallen off the mattress. "J.B., I'm a guest here. What will Barbara and Thack think if I . . ." Her voice trailed away as she searched for delicate phrasing.

"If you spend the days in their house and the nights in mine?" he finished for her.

"Yes," she murmured, glancing away from the brilliance of his eyes.

"They'll think we're lovers," he said quietly. "And we are."

"I know, but . . ." Again her voice failed.

"But what?" he persisted. "Are you ashamed of being my lover?"

"No!" Nicole forced him upright as she reared up, unmindful of her nakedness. "But how will Barbara and Thack react?" she asked. "And Aunt Ellie!" She groaned.

J.B. snorted. "Aunt Ellie will likely make noises about me making an honest woman of you by offering marriage," he said dryly. "You want to get married?" he added, raising one eyebrow.

"Of course not!" Nicole said, denying an inner voice that cried, *Yes, yes.* She shook her head, not to reinforce her refusal but to dispel the inner voice.

Leaning forward, J.B. kissed her hard, quickly. "But you do want to continue to be with me like this?" he whispered, smiling when she tried to recapture his mouth with her own.

"You know I do." Nicole sighed when he kissed her again.

"I'll talk to Thack," he said decisively, easing her down onto the bed. "And you talk to Barbara." When she opened her mouth to question him further, he very effectively silenced her.

Nicole fell asleep snug in J.B.'s embrace, secure in the warmth of his body and the weight of his thigh pinning hers to the mattress.

The sunshine of a hot Texas morning woke her. Yawning and stretching luxuriously, she discovered she was alone in the huge circular bed. J.B. had gone to work and might very well be having a man-to-man talk with Thack at that very moment, she thought.

Groaning, Nicole dragged her tired, pleasantly aching body from the bed. Now it was her turn. She had to talk to Barbara, to try to explain a situation she wasn't at all sure she understood herself.

But first she'd change the bedding and straighten up the house!

Six

Busywork!

A grin spreading across her face, Nicole paused in the act of snapping the enormous top sheet over the round bed. The tiny voice of her conscience had whispered the chiding accusation at her several times during the hour since she'd awakened and remembered that she had to talk to Barbara.

What would Barbara think of her houseguest spending the night with her ranch foreman? Nicole wondered as she smoothed the green-and-white spread over the bed. A soft sigh whispered through Nicole's lips as she turned to survey the room. A tingle zigzagged through her when her gaze returned to the bed. With stark honesty Nicole admitted that she'd spent the most exciting, most satisfying and happiest hours of her twenty-eight years in that bed with Josh Barnet.

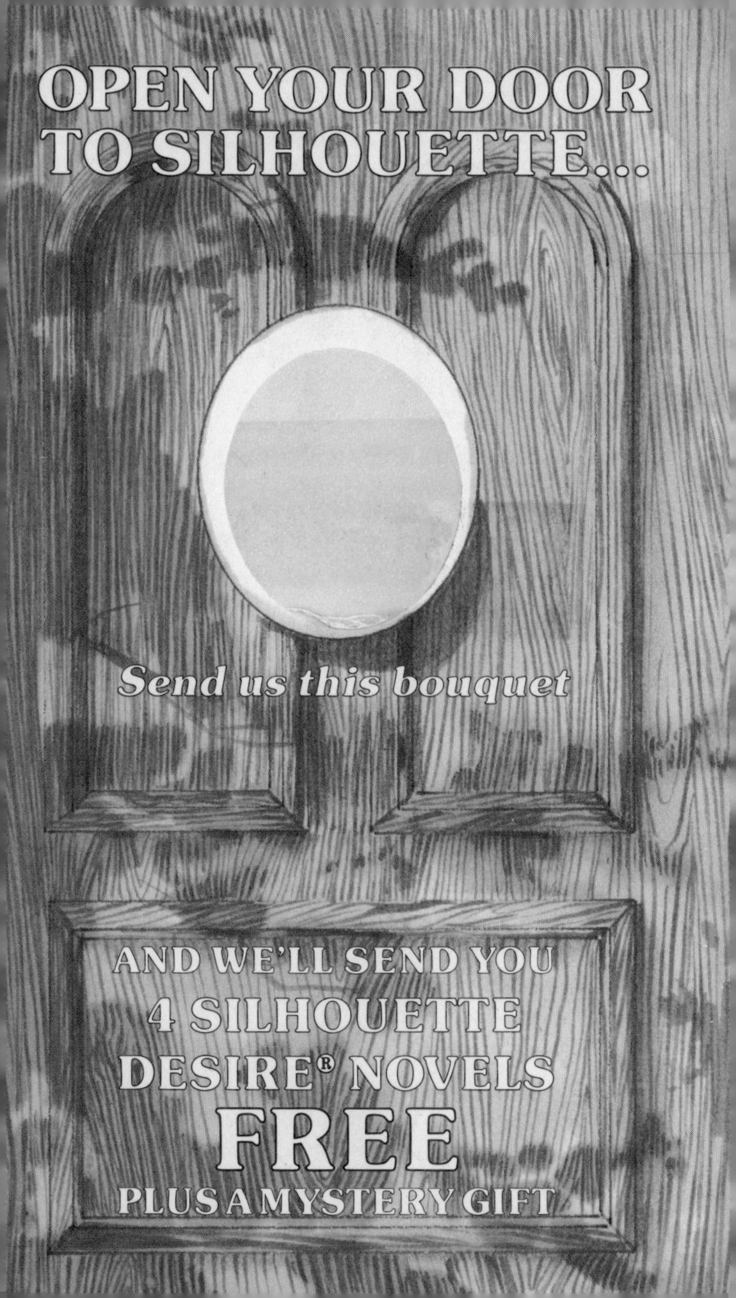

OPEN YOUR DOOR
TO SILHOUETTE...
Send us this bouquet
AND WE'LL SEND YOU
4 SILHOUETTE
DESIRE® NOVELS
FREE
PLUS A MYSTERY GIFT

NOW THAT THE DOOR IS OPEN . . .
Peel off the bouquet and send it on the postpaid order card to receive:

4 FREE BOOKS
from
Silhouette ❤ *Desire*®

And a mystery gift as an extra bonus!

MONEY-SAVING HOME DELIVERY!

Once you receive your 4 FREE books and gift, you'll be able to open your door to more great romance reading month after month. Enjoy the convenience of previewing 6 brand-new books every month delivered right to your home months before they appear in stores. Each book is yours for only $2.25—.25¢ less than the retail price, plus .69¢ postage and handling per shipment.

NO-RISK GUARANTEE!

—There's no obligation to buy—and the free books and gift are yours to keep forever.
— You pay the lowest price possible and receive books months before they appear in stores.
— You may end your subscription anytime—just write and let us know.

RETURN THE POSTPAID ORDER CARD TODAY AND OPEN YOUR DOOR TO THESE 4 EXCITING LOVE-FILLED NOVELS. THEY ARE YOURS ABSOLUTELY FREE ALONG WITH YOUR MYSTERY GIFT.

Extra FREE BONUS!

When you return the postpaid order card with the bouquet attached, you'll also receive a FREE surprise gift! Send for yours today.

Remember . . .

To receive your 4 FREE books and mystery gift, return the postpaid card below. But don't delay!

DETACH AND MAIL CARD TODAY

If offer card below is missing, write to:
If offer card is missing, write to: Silhouette Books, P.O. Box 609, Fort Erie, Ontario, L2A 5X3.

Merely thinking of him increased the tingle to a quiver. And now Nicole knew why the family called J.B. the hombre—for he definitely was one macho man!

Assailed by warm, sensuous weakness, Nicole lay back on the bed, reliving the hours she had spent in J.B.'s arms. Memory flashing, her breathing grew shallow, and the lower part of her body felt heavy and achingly empty. Into her mind crept the comparison she had made between J.B. and Jason Norwich, the only men ever in her life. It was ironic that they shared the same first-name initial. Jason was wine; J.B. was water—life giving, life sustaining.

From her supine position Nicole gazed at the abundance of hanging plants. Water; J.B. Yes. A soft smile curved her lips. J.B. was as fundamental as water, and as necessary. But he possessed other qualities, as well. He was as fiery as the sun, as volatile as the wind, as enduring as the very earth he had sprung from. Nicole had no idea how she knew all these things to be true of J.B.; she only knew they were. And this man had made her, however briefly, a part of himself. The very memory of that joining was delicious!

Suddenly Nicole wanted him again, then, at once. She wanted him to stride into the room, toss off his clothes, tear off hers and make love to her—gently, roughly, passionately, tenderly, and not necessarily in that order!

A longing sigh was wrenched from Nicole's throat. She had to get up, get moving. She had a friend to face and an explanation to make. J.B. had not hesitated getting on with the business of everyday living; she should not be hesitating, either. The night was over.

The sun was shining on a new day. It was past time for her to get it together.

I will. Nicole rolled onto her side and snuggled into the spread as she made the silent decision.

You're crazy. J.B. silently mocked himself as he handed the reins of his horse over to the bandy-legged hostler.

"Back early, ain't ya?" Sean Legs Ryan observed, turning to lead the Morgan into the stable. At sixty-seven, most people had forgotten the man's Christian name; he was simply Legs and accepted by everyone as—in Thack's words—"the best damned horse handler this side of the big river."

"I need the truck," J.B. lied easily. "Decided I might as well grab something for lunch other than a cold sandwich while I'm here." He tossed the impromptu excuse at Legs as he headed for the small house. There was no response from the other man; J.B. hadn't expected any. Legs was already inside the stable, doing what he did best.

As he drew close to the house, J.B. pulled the broad-brimmed straw hat from his head and wiped his face on his shirtsleeve. He felt hot and sticky. His throat was bone-dry. A smile twitched his lips as he settled the hat back onto his disheveled hair. His discomfort had precious little to do with the hot sun of midday in late June. J.B. liked the heat. He had been born and raised in the glaring Texas sunlight.

Approaching the shaded porch of his home, J.B. acknowledged his uncomfortable condition for exactly what it was; Josh Barnet was *hot* for a woman, not from prevailing weather conditions.

As they had set off in different directions that morning, J.B. on horseback, Thack in one of the four-wheel-drive vehicles, J.B. had been spared the inevitable lecture from his friend-employer. Memory had not been as kind as fate. Throughout the long morning, while working the Morgan through the low hills and gullies flushing out strays and mavericks, J.B.'s body and mind had bombarded him with living-color memories of the night before.

Reaching for the door latch, J.B. concluded that the strength of the Texas summer sun paled in comparison to the blast of raw heat generated by one Pennsylvania woman with a faint but somehow endearing scar on one cheek.

And he was crazy for hurrying back on the lame-brained excuse of a change in the usual lunch menu, J.B. mused as he moved noiselessly into the cool house. Nicole had probably returned to the main house, and all he was likely to get *was* a change in menu.

His broad, flatly muscled chest heaving in a silent sigh, J.B. started for the tiny kitchen next to the living room. A vivid memory of how alluring Nicole had looked curled up asleep in his bed at four-thirty that morning halted his stride opposite the bedroom door. Dressing in work clothes and leaving the room had been one of the hardest duties J.B. had ever had to perform.

Though reluctant to view his excitingly rumpled yet now empty bed, J.B. slowly walked to the closed narrow door. Deciding he harbored latent masochistic tendencies, he quietly turned the knob, gently pushed the door open and felt a fresh gust of heat rush into his body while all the air rushed out. As if waiting for him, Nicole, *his* Nicole, lay curled up in the very center of his bed!

Nicole didn't hear J.B.; she *felt* him. Without warning life and warmth began to hum through her body, whispering of erotic delights to come, singing in praise of his prowess. Closing her eyes, Nicole drew a slow, deep breath. He was in the room. She just knew it. And if she was wrong, she'd just die!

"Hi." Nicole murmured the low greeting as she opened her eyes and rolled onto her back. In work-worn jeans and faded shirt, J.B. was infinitely more appetizing than the most exotic cuisine prepared by a master chef. Merely looking at him created a ravenous hunger inside her.

"Hi, yourself." J.B.'s beautiful voice, raspy with need, flicked at the hunger gnawing at Nicole. As he moved silently into the room, his gaze caressed her body before sweeping over the neatly made bed. "I liked it better the way it looked this morning," he murmured, a smile tilting his lips, "all rumpled with the proof of a satisfying night."

"But the night is gone." Nicole was unsurprised to find speech difficult. J.B. had halted near her legs at the side curve of the bed; his fingers were busy undoing shirt buttons! "It's...it's lunchtime!" she squeaked, eyes widening as, the shirt falling open, his hand dropped to his belt.

"Damned if it ain't," he drawled, sliding jeans and dark briefs down his flanks before perching on the edge of the bed to tug pants, boots and socks from his body. "All the better to see you, my dear," he quoted, slanting a sideways, sexy-as-the-devil look at her. Then, his eyes glittering with a potent mixture of desire and deviltry, he chided, "I think you're over-

Moving with unnatural jerkiness, Thack crossed the room and dropped like a stone onto a deeply cushioned chair. "J.B. handed his horse over to Legs around noon. No one has seen hide nor hair of him since," he muttered.

"So?" Barbara asked quietly.

"So?" Thack barked. "So it seems pretty clear that J.B. spent the night and a damned big chunk of the day with Nicole!" His fingers again brushed through his hair. "What in hell are they up to?"

Though Barbara clapped a hand over her mouth, she wasn't completely successful in muffling her laughter. "Oh, Thackery!" she choked. "I don't believe you actually said that!"

"Don't get cute, Barb," Thack warned, fighting a grin.

"I know we've recently had a baby and our love life has been on hold, so to speak, but surely it hasn't been *that* long since . . ." Barbara's voice gave way to more laughter.

"You're lookin' for trouble, Barbara, honey," Thack warned again, this time losing the battle against a grin. "Okay, I *know* what they're doing. That's what bothers me."

"But, darling, why?" Crossing to him, Barbara sat on his lap and curled her arms around his neck. "J.B. is like a brother to you. And Nicole's the closest thing to a sister I've ever had. They have both been through a hell we can only imagine. If they can give each other happiness, if only in a physical way, why should we interfere?"

"I don't want to interfere, honey," Thack said tiredly. "All I want from this life is to love my wife and baby and provide for them by working my spread."

He lifted a finger to seal her lips when she parted them to respond. "But I love that man, Barb. I love J.B. as much as I do my twin, Zack. And I like your friend. I just don't want to see either J.B. or Nicole part company hurting even more than they already do."

Barbara looked thoughtful as she worried her bottom lip with her teeth for a few moments, then asked, "And you're afraid they will hurt each other?"

Thack heaved a deep sigh. "Hell, honey, I don't know. But look at it unemotionally. They are both handicapped, if in different ways. They both need partners strong enough to deal with the psychological wounds as well as the physical scars." He moved his shoulders in a half shrug. "You tell me. Except for sexual release, can they help each other? Or will they hurt each other even more?"

Barbara's hazel eyes shimmered with tears. "Oh, Thack, I don't know!" she cried, hugging him fiercely in a bid for reassurance. "All I was thinking about was now, this moment, and the obvious attraction they feel for one another. They have both suffered so cruelly." The tears escaped to slide unnoticed down her face. "I was happy to believe they found pleasure in one another."

Thack noticed her tears. Smiling tenderly, he gently brushed the wet streaks from her cheeks. "And maybe they have," he consoled her softly. "I suppose that all we can do is wait and see. And be here for them if they need us."

"Need something?" J.B. breathed against the curve of Nicole's neck the instant she opened her eyes.

"For instance?" she asked, pulling away to eye him warily.

"Food? Water?" Smiling, he curled the gloved hand around her breast, enjoying her response to the rough leather, even though he was denied the sensation himself. "A little loving?"

"A little loving!" Nicole exclaimed, staring at him in amazement. "Good grief, man! Don't you ever get tired?"

"Sure." Sliding his hand away from her, J.B. rolled onto his back, then stretched widely. "I get tired mending fence and digging postholes and searching out cows that don't want to be found. I get tired from bouncing on a hard saddle." Turning his head on the pillow, he gave her a long, slow smile. "I even got tired a little while ago, right here in this bed. But I'm not tired now."

"How old are you?" Peering at him, Nicole examined the creases radiating from the corners of his eyes and the lines bracketing his mouth.

"I'm sneaking up on forty," J.B. answered in a coolly unperturbed tone.

Nicole grinned. "Sneaking?"

J.B. shrugged. "I figure if I sneak up on it, maybe nobody'll notice."

"I see." Her grin gave way to laughter. "I think."

"How old are you?"

Nicole studied his somber expression as J.B. examined her face in turn. "Twenty-eight," she said, echoing his coolness.

"Incredible."

"Twenty-eight is incredible?" Nicole laughed.

"No, not twenty-eight," J.B. said seriously. "Your beauty. Even with the scar, your face is so beautiful it's incredible."

Nicole froze and fought against a welling feeling of sickness. *Not him. Oh, please, not him, too!* The cry was silent, a painful scream of protest pounding in her head. J.B.'s gaze was like a caress on each of her features, a caress she could not endure. Moving slowly, as if in fear of breaking, Nicole turned away to stare at the wall.

J.B.'s sudden indrawn breath was loud in the silence of the room. "What is it, Nicole?" Concern was evident in his soft voice. "What's wrong? Do you feel sick?" Gently, firmly, he caught her quivering chin in the inanimate palm and forced her to look at him again. "Tell me, dammit!" he ordered at the sight of her too bright eyes and her colorless face.

"Yes!" Nicole shouted. "Yes, I feel sick! I am sick to death of hearing about my *beauty*!"

"What?" J.B.'s tone and expression went completely blank. "What are you talking about?"

"Beauty!" Nicole retorted, her lip curling in a sneer. "I've heard every possible compliment: beautiful, lovely, gorgeous, superb, stunning. You name it, I've heard every damned one!" She had to pause to draw breath into her shaking body, then she lashed out again, cutting him off as he opened his mouth to speak. "It's a *face*, skin, bones—a facade! I have been very fortunate. I'm the product of a long line of extremely attractive people. But have you, has anyone, ever paused to wonder if there might be some kind of intelligent life hiding behind the *beautiful* mask?" Her voice danced close to the edge of control. "I seriously doubt it!" she finished, raising her hands to cover her face and muffle the sobs tearing at her throat.

There was dead silence from the space beside her on the bed. A silence stark in contrast to the storm wreaking havoc on Nicole. Then a moan, and a whisper raw with understanding and empathy.

"Oh, damn."

Lying beside her, close but separate, it felt to J.B. as if each sob from Nicole's throat stabbed into his chest like a knife. *I won't touch her. I won't touch her.* Gritting his teeth, he repeated the phrase to himself like a litany. Then he closed his eyes, defeated. *The hell I won't!* With great care J.B. drew her into his arms, cradling her thin, trembling body against the muscular strength of his own. Stroking her back, her shoulders, her hair, he absorbed her pain into his body and mind and heart.

J.B. allowed Nicole ten minutes to vent a lifetime of insecurity. Then, raising her tear-streaked face, he smiled into her filmy eyes and tapped his forefinger against her temple.

"Hey!" He spoke in a conspiratorial murmur. "Is there any intelligent life in there?"

Emotions churned to the surface. Nicole swung from the depths of one to the heights of another. She dissolved into laughter.

"I like to think so," she sniffed, drawing back to wipe ineffectually at her wet cheeks. "But, please, don't call your bookie on it."

"Bookie?" Easing up to sit cross-legged beside her, J.B. managed to look both shocked and stern. "Gambling is illegal, and I might remind you that you are speaking to a former officer of the law."

Sublimely unconscious of their nudity, Nicole stared at him somberly and drew the back of her hand across her nose. "I know." She sniffed again. "And I want to discuss the subject with you in depth sometime. But right now you wouldn't happen to have a tissue handy, would you?''

Laughing, J.B. sprang from the tangled bed-clothes. Shirttails flapping against his naked flanks, he strode to the double dresser. Yanking open the top drawer, he plucked a white handkerchief from inside, then leaving the drawer open, he returned to the curved side of the bed to hand it to her.

"I'm going to take a shower while you mop up in here," he said, smiling softly. "Okay?"

Dabbing at her nose, Nicole began to nod. She stopped abruptly to stare pleadingly up at him. "I suppose you wouldn't consider letting me join you in the shower, would you?" she asked hopefully.

Bending over her, J.B. brushed his mouth over her tear-wet lips. "You suppose correctly," he murmured.

"You're going to take it off, aren't you?"

"Yes."

"I could help you with it." She didn't mention the contraption by name; she didn't have to.

"No." Sliding the gloved hand under her chin, J.B. gently lifted her head. "Not yet, Nicki. It's too soon." He paused, then admitted rawly, "I know you can face it. But, you see, I can't."

Nicole blinked at a fresh surge of tears as his arm fell back to his side and he turned away from her. His hand was on the bathroom doorknob when her soft call stopped him. "J.B.?"

"Mmm?" J.B. glanced at her over his shoulder.

"We know each other at the most intimate level," she said in an aching whisper. "And yet we—"

"I know," he interrupted gently. "I feel positive I'd like the intelligent life hiding behind the mask." His smile was wry. "The question is, have you any interest in getting to know a one-armed ex-cop?" Feeling an exposure that had nothing whatever to do with his naked body, J.B. held his breath. It wasn't necessary to hold it very long—Nicole answered immediately, emphatically.

"Yes."

J.B. stared at her for a moment while a slow smile grew to soften the unrelenting harshness of his features. "I have two weeks' vacation time due," he said. "Will you go away with me?" This time he barely had time to draw breath before she answered.

"Yes."

"When?" he shot back. "Tomorrow? Tonight?"

Nicole's smile held sheer pleasure. "What's wrong with right now?"

Laughter rumbling in his chest, J.B. relaxed his death grip on the doorknob. "Not a damned thing." He grinned. "There are just a few minor details, namely your friend Barbara and my boss, Thack. And the simple fact that we both need a hot shower and a solid meal." Striding back to her, he swept her into his arms. Crushing her to him, he kissed her deeply. "Whoa!" he said as he released her. "We'll leave tomorrow . . . early."

"Very early," Nicole called after him breathlessly as he loped into the bathroom.

The phone rang in the living room forty minutes later while they were working together to restore order to the tangled bedding. Though they were both showered and fully dressed, Nicole had insisted on straightening the bed before giving consideration to a meal. J.B. had agreed reluctantly, grumbling all the while about the prospect of starvation since he had relinquished lunch in favor of appeasing a stronger appetite.

"Thack," J.B. muttered as the phone rang.

"Barbara!" Nicole groaned repentantly, trailing him into the living room.

They were both wrong. Standing inches from the phone, Nicole could clearly hear Aunt Ellie's tart voice.

"You two idiots have exactly five minutes to get over here for dinner. If you're not here by then, I'll feed your supper to the hogs!"

"Yes, ma'am," J.B. said meekly, grinning rakishly at Nicole. A wince wiped away his grin when the sound of Ellie slamming down the phone reached his ear.

"She means business," Nicole observed, fighting laughter. "Doesn't she?"

"Naw," J.B. shrugged confidently. "We don't keep any hogs."

Hands clasped, and laughing together like teenagers, they strolled through the soft dusk to the main house.

"Are you sure you're doing the right thing, Nicole?"

"No." Nicole carefully placed a neatly folded blouse in the suitcase before glancing up at Barbara. Four hours had passed since Nicole and J.B. had returned to the main house, four hours in which Barbara had somehow managed to contain the questions roused by J.B.'s cool announcement about the vacation. "But then—" Nicole shrugged "—I'm not sure I'm doing the wrong thing, either."

"I'm positive you'll be perfectly safe," Barbara said quickly. "I have no doubt about that. But two weeks? Nicole, you know so little about each other." Certain she was stating her position inadequately, Barbara sighed and sank onto the bed, shoulders drooping. "I adore J.B., but . . ."

"But you can't help worrying, I know." Pushing the case aside, Nicole sat down beside her friend. "I'm a little worried myself," she admitted on a shaky laugh. "J.B.'s even more complex than I originally thought," Nicole explained when Barbara frowned. "He fascinates me." She wet her dry lips, then confessed, "He also pleases me, in more than a physical way." She lifted her shoulders helplessly. "I don't know how to explain it exactly. Perhaps I've been more lonely than I realized." She sighed. "All I know is that I want this time with him."

"I just don't want you to get hurt." Reaching out impulsively, Barbara clasped Nicole's hand. "Neither does Thack. I can tell you that he is not at all happy about this."

Nicole laughed, naturally, easily. "Thack made his position very clear before, during and after dinner." She shook her head. "For a while there I was really afraid he was going to take a swing at J.B."

"So was I." Barbara made a sour face. "Men are so . . . so physical."

"Yes." Nicole's smile was wry. "It was obvious that J.B. would have been happy to accommodate Thack. And they're friends!" She raised her hands, then let them drop. "I shudder to think of what might have happened if they were enemies."

"Do men ever grow up completely, I wonder?" Barbara murmured.

"You're asking the wrong woman!" Nicole laughed. "My experience with men has been extremely limited."

"Which is why I'm concerned," Barbara said, bringing the conversation full circle.

Nicole's eyes darkened as her laughter faded. "And I appreciate your concern," she replied sincerely. "But I feel I must find out some things about J.B. and about myself." Her smile betrayed a lack of certainty. "You see, Barbara, I have a feeling that I could love him." She held up her hand to stop Barbara from interrupting her. "I mean really love him, not the childish infatuation I felt for Jason. And, in all honesty, it's frightening." Standing, Nicole calmly resumed packing. "In a way I can't explain, J.B. is frightening. And yet I need to find out, explore what it is that has drawn us to one another." She gazed bleakly at Barbara. "Does that make any sense at all?"

"Yes." Rising, Barbara began folding a lacy black teddy. "Thack probably wouldn't understand, but I do." She handed the filmy garment to Nicole, then smiled. "So you're going to his family's summer home at Lake Possum Kingdom?"

Sighing her relief, Nicole nodded. "By way of his father's ranch. His excuse for stopping is to pick up the keys to the lake house."

"Excuse?" Barbara raised her eyebrows. "Excuse for what?"

"Well, I may be wrong." Nicole frowned. "I certainly have been before. But I believe J.B. wants me to meet his family."

"But that's good!" Barbara exclaimed. "Isn't it?"

"At this point in the relationship?" Nicole retorted. "Damned if I know!"

*   *   *

The sky was still a soft predawn pink when Barbara and Thack stood, arms linked, watching the trail of dust created by J.B.'s car.

"I still don't like it." Thack's voice was gritty.

Tilting her head, Barbara smiled up into her husband's handsome face. "I don't recall anybody asking if you approved or not."

Thack's eyes narrowed. "I know, but dammit, why did J.B. feel the need to get away to be with Nicole?" His tone held a hint of injury. "Hell, honey, this has been his home for years!"

"Thackery, really!" Barbara exclaimed. "They want to have some time together alone. Surely you can understand that?"

Shifting his gaze from the now empty ranch road, Thack grinned down at his wife. "Yeah, okay, I get the message. I've been there. I can understand that."

Seven

The private road leading to the Barnet ranch seemed endless. An arcing plume of yellow dust marked the passage of the car. Inside the vehicle, the air-conditioning fought valiantly against the intense heat. If she had learned nothing else during her trip to the state, Nicole had absorbed the fact that Texas was hot in June.

Except for a forty-five-minute stop for breakfast, they had driven straight through from the Sharp property to J.B.'s father's spread northwest of Fort Worth. Though unstrained, the conversation between Nicole and J.B. had centered on the country-side they traveled through. Surprisingly, J.B. was a font of information, not only about the hill country and the area surrounding his birthplace outside Fort Worth but also about the entire state of Texas.

Fascinated by both the man seated beside her and the landscape beyond the car windows, Nicole barely noticed the passage of time. It was still morning, if late morning, when he drove the sports car—another surprise for Nicole—under the arched metal sign proclaiming the domain of Austin Barnet.

"Your father was named for Stephen Austin?" Nicole asked, twisting in the bucket seat to glance back at the sign through the rear window.

"Yeah." J.B. shot a grin at her. "My brother, too."

Settling back in her seat, Nicole turned to gaze at him. "You have a brother?"

"Hmmm."

"You didn't mention him."

J.B. laughed. "We've only known each other a couple of days. I didn't mention a lot of things." His blue eyes warmed as he slid a glance over her. "I thought that was the point of this trip."

Among other things, Nicole thought, trying to hide her smile from him. "Any other siblings?" she inquired blandly.

J.B. shook his head. "No, just the one brother. Steve's forty-four, six years older than I am." The car bounced, and he eased his foot from the accelerator, then sliced a look at her. "What about you? Any brothers or sisters?"

"Like you, I have one brother." Nicole smiled. "Coincidentally, you and Peter are the same age." Her smile slid into a teasing grin. "And you're both a lot older than I."

"Ten years is not a big deal, honey," J.B. grunted, failing in an attempt to appear unconcerned. "Is it?"

Nicole thought about letting him stew for a while, then relented when his eyebrows drew together in a frown. "No, J.B., ten years are not a big deal."

"I'm delighted to hear you say it," he drawled, bringing the car to a stop in the curved driveway in front of a low, rambling ranch house. "Even though it wouldn't have changed my position either way." Tossing a grin at her over his shoulder, he pushed open his door and unfolded his long form from behind the wheel.

As Nicole moved to follow suit, a tall, full-figured woman stepped onto the low step before the front door.

"Josh is here, Austin," the woman called back over her shoulder. Then she was striding along the walkway to the curved drive, hands extended to J.B. "You've lost weight, son," she said, then laughed with delight as J.B. grasped one outstretched hand to pull her into an embrace.

"And you've gained some," J.B. chided, smacking her gently on one padded hip. "But you're still the best-lookin' woman around, Mom." Drawing back, he examined her flushed, smiling face. "How are you?" he asked in a low, loving tone.

"Bossy as ever." The gravelly voiced observation came from the doorway, from a man as tall and as whipcord lean as J.B. The man, obviously J.B.'s father, resumed speaking as he ambled toward them. "It's about time you decided to visit. Your mother's been complaining for weeks about not hearing from you."

Nicole felt Austin Barnet's sharp-eyed gaze as he swept a speculative look over her. Feeling very accurately summed up, her cheeks grew warm when he sliced an appreciative glance at his son.

"How do you always manage to latch on to the best-lookin' women?" Austin asked dryly, grasping the hand J.B. extended.

As one of his slow, exciting smiles played over his lips, J.B. gazed at his mother, then at Nicole, then to the front doorway. "The talent must be hereditary," he replied solemnly. "Both Steve and I seem to have inherited it." His smile softened. "Hello, Leona. Come give me a hug and meet my lady."

The color deepening in her cheeks at his term for her, Nicole shifted her gaze to the young woman hovering shyly in the doorway. As the woman came forward, Nicole gasped silently. Leona was lovely in the way particular to women of Latin blood, with a mass of shiny black hair, an enviable creamy complexion and dark sloe eyes. Nicole guessed her age to be twenty-two or twenty-three.

During the ensuing introductions Nicole realized why J.B. had been insistent about the insignificance of the ten years' difference in their ages. Leona was Steve Barnet's wife and at least twenty years his junior. As the group slowly made its way into the house, Nicole wondered what J.B.'s brother was like. She was to find out very soon.

"So you're headed up to the lake?"

J.B.'s family seemed to focus on the answer to Austin's question. In much the same manner as a few days previously, Nicole had been shown to a bathroom where she could freshen up, then urged to join the family in the kitchen for the lunch Maryanne Barnet had waiting.

"That's right," J.B. murmured from where he was standing. Arching an eyebrow at Nicole in question, he lifted the electric coffeepot with his good hand. At her nod, he poured a stream of the aromatic brew into a delicate china cup, then continued speaking as he delivered the cup to where Nicole was seated at the table. "Since I had the vacation time coming, I decided to show the lake house to Nicole." He hesitated for an instant, then stared into his father's shrewd gray eyes. "Any objections?"

The elder Barnet's grin revealed crooked but still white teeth. "No. It's your house."

"Not yet," J.B. retorted as he sat down. "And not for a long time to come."

"Please God!" Maryanne concurred.

"Yes," Leona murmured.

Nicole glanced from one to the other and wondered what in the world they were talking about. She was about to ask when a new voice rang through the house.

"Where are they?"

"In the kitchen, where else?" Austin shouted.

Nicole glanced at J.B. just as another tall, slender Barnet strode into the room. Here the resemblance was strong, the difference being in the twenty pounds Steve had on his younger brother. As J.B. stood, Steve rounded the table and clasped him in a fierce bear hug.

"Damn, boy!" Steve fairly growled as he put J.B. from him. "You've got some kind of power in your arms. When are you goin' back to work?"

Already confused, Nicole was puzzled by the question. J.B. worked for Thack—didn't he? The silence that came over the assemblage wasn't nearly as unsettling as the expression that came over J.B.'s face.

"You looking for a rap in the mouth, big brother?" he asked too softly.

Steve merely chuckled. "Watch it, boy, you'll scare the hell out of me." Moving with slow deliberation, he turned to stare at Nicole. "Well, now, what have we here?" he murmured.

Unaffected, J.B. tried to look bored. "Nicole, in case you haven't guessed, this is my brother, Steve, the family idiot." He gave his brother a mocking smile. "Steve, Nicole Vanzant."

Standing to her full, considerable height, Nicole flashed the smile that had helped make her famous in the world of modeling. Poised as she was, she might have been attired in haute couture instead of faded jeans and an electric-blue T-shirt.

"I'm delighted to meet you, Steve." The hand that swallowed hers was surprisingly gentle; the eyes that drilled into hers were amazingly shrewd. Nicole maintained her poise as Steve lowered his gaze to examine the scar on her face.

"Not nearly as delighted as I am to meet you, I'll bet," he finally responded, releasing her hand. He smiled sweetly when she arched a quizzical eyebrow. "It's been awhile since J.B. thought enough of a woman to bring her here," he explained. "You must be a very special lady."

Did J.B. regard her as a very special lady? The question tantalized Nicole throughout the hours they spent at the ranch. It was only one of many questions that teased her mind. Biding her time until they were alone again, Nicole relaxed and enjoyed the visit. Long before they left the ranch to resume their trip to the lake, Nicole decided that J.B.'s family was well worth meeting. Plainspoken and down-to-earth, the

Barnets, like the Sharps, were genuinely nice people and fun to be with. Nicole could not help but wonder if her life would have been entirely different had her own family possessed the same kind of open affection and camaraderie.

"Well, what do you think?" J.B. asked before they had reached the end of the long, private road.

"About what?" Nicole replied, knowing full well what he was referring to.

J.B. sent her a mocking look. "You know what," he chided. "The assortment of Barnets, of course."

"It's an excellent assortment," Nicole mocked back. "Your mother is a warm, loving woman. Your father's a pushover underneath his gruff exterior. And, like you, Steve is the natural result of those two good people, prickly on the outside and tender on the inside." She paused, envisioning the seemingly shy, dark-eyed beauty married to his brother, then added contemplatively, "And Leona's a quiet tiger with claws sheathed."

"Very astute," J.B. drawled the praise in an attempt to conceal his surprise. "And right on target. My mother is the most loving person I've ever known. My dad's a caring man. And Leona is a tigress when circumstances warrant, usually in defense of my brother." He slanted a look at her. "So you think Steve and I are prickly, eh?"

Nicole smiled into his narrowed gaze. "On the outside, yes," she said complacently.

"And tender underneath?" he persisted.

"Uh-huh," she murmured, beginning to grin.

J.B. grinned with her. "I surely do hope so, ma'am. I would've made a lousy cop, never mind person, otherwise."

Suddenly alert, Nicole grasped the opening. "And were you a good cop?"

"Yes."

Nicole liked his quick response; actually, she liked J.B., period. Strangely, liking him didn't make sleeping with him easier—it made it harder. If one liked a person, one cared about that person, and caring could get a woman hurt. Nicole imagined she could already feel the pang of despair she'd suffer when her vacation was over and they parted.

"Come back, Nicole." J.B.'s voice was low but carried a definite command. "You're with me now."

Mentally shaking off the thought of future pain, Nicole tried to respond with a casualness she was far from feeling. "And does being with you mean I'm allowed no private thoughts?" she inquired sweetly.

"Not if those thoughts are about another man," he answered in a tight, controlled tone.

"But I wasn't thinking about another man," she protested, thinking *at least, not directly.*

"Good thing," he grunted. "Because I'm very possessive, lady."

Lady. Come meet my lady. Yes, she mused, J.B. was indeed a possessive man, and Nicole was unsurprised by that fact. What did surprise her was the realization that she was beginning to feel possessive of him, too. She knew danger lay in that direction—a very real danger of losing her heart to a man who had as many, if not more, psychological quirks than she had.

Lord! It would be like the blind leading the blind, she thought, feeling the first of the pangs of hurt.

"What are you thinking?" J.B. demanded more than asked.

Nicole hesitated, staring sightlessly at the terrain, which was changing from hills to low mountains. Then, avoiding his locked-tight profile, she muttered, "I was thinking of you and me as the blind leading the blind."

J.B.'s response was instantaneous. "Or the newly sighted supporting the newly sighted."

Carefully, slowly, Nicole turned to look at him. "And how do we become newly sighted?"

"By baring our souls to one another," J.B. answered with hard determination.

Suddenly uncertain of the wisdom of spending two weeks with him, Nicole shifted uncomfortably in the confining seat. "You're willing to do that?" she asked in a dry tone.

"I thought getting to know one another was the reason for going away together," he answered.

"Nothing was said about baring souls," Nicole retorted. "I guess I assumed it would be more the baring of bodies."

J.B. slowed the car to make a turn onto a side road, from which could be seen a portion of the lake. Keeping a steady gaze on the winding road, he observed wryly, "Hell, we've done that." A slow smile worked its way across his lips. "And I'm looking forward to repeating the performance."

Nicole wanted to feel annoyed. She wanted to feel impatient. She wanted to feel upset. She felt none of the negative emotions. What she did feel was an embarrassing urgency to repeat the performance and a desire to avoid thinking about the baring of souls.

"We're here."

J.B.'s soft statement startled Nicole. She was so involved with her thoughts she hadn't noticed that they'd arrived. "How lovely!" she exclaimed, glancing first at the single-story dwelling, then at the wind-ruffled blue water of the lake. "What did you call it?"

"Possum Kingdom." Shoving his door open, J.B. stepped from the car, then grunted with pleasure as he stretched. "This place was *my* hideout after I got released from the hospital."

Alighting from the car, Nicole gazed at him over the low roof. "Your equivalent to the Maine coast?" Her attempt at a tone of light humor failed dismally, foiled by memories too fresh to be handled lightly.

"Exactly." J.B.'s solemn expression spoke eloquently of long days and longer nights. "Whereas you sought comfort on the shoreline of an ocean, I drew mine from the shore of this lake." His thin lips curved in a wry smile. "There is something soothing about moving water, isn't there?"

"Yes." Nicole's gaze drifted to the waves ruffling the surface of the lake. "Soothing and healing," she murmured, as if to herself.

"Would you like to see the inside of the house?"

J.B.'s quiet voice drew her attention away from the undulating water. "Yes, of course," she replied and stepped briskly to the rear of the car to assist him with the luggage.

The inside of the house was much more spacious than it appeared from the outside. Entering a compact foyer, J.B. explained the layout tersely with brief hand motions. To the right was a small powder room, to the left an open railed landing that led into a short hallway at the bottom of three shallow steps. The stairs descended directly into a huge square living room with sliding glass doors that gave access to a screened deck and a panoramic view of the mountain-edged lake. To the right of the shallow stairs ran a long breakfast bar that separated the narrow kitchen from the living room. At the far end of the kitchen, a large area had been designated as the dining room, with wide windows overlooking the lake. No walls or partitions separated one area from another. The architecture was open, the decor relaxing.

With a barely perceptible flick of his gloved hand, J.B. indicated the white brick wall at the far left of the living room, most of which was taken up by a wide fireplace. At the very end of the wall was a door.

"My parents' bedroom is through that door," J.B. said. "The room has a private bath." Raising his hand, he indicated the railed hallway overlooking the living room. "There are two bedrooms and a full bath along that hallway."

"And one of those bedrooms is yours?" Nicole guessed, planning to request the other room for herself.

"No," he said, turning to circle around the end of the breakfast bar. "My room's back this way."

Startled, Nicole followed him through a doorway in the compact kitchen that led into a mudroom, which was really no larger than a wide passageway. The half room contained a washer and a dryer, a freezer chest and cases of beer and soda stacked next to a wooden wine rack. The room also contained three shallow steps that led up to an open door.

Nicole trailed J.B. up the stairs and across the threshold, then came to an abrupt halt. The room that should have been a double garage was enormous and had been turned into a luxurious apartment.

"This is yours?" she asked, glancing around curiously.

"Yes." Dropping their cases unceremoniously, J.B. turned to her. "*Ours* for the next two weeks." Then, as if he knew exactly what she was thinking, he stared into her eyes, daring her to ask for one of the other bedrooms.

Chin raised, Nicole stared back defiantly. "Am I supposed to feel intimidated?" she asked, hoping to dispel that very sensation by stating it aloud. Though she didn't know quite what to expect, Nicole never expected him to laugh. Yet that was exactly what J.B. did do, freely, richly.

"I guess that was my intent," he admitted when his laughter subsided. Walking over to her, he took the small suitcase from her hand but didn't set it aside. "I'm sorry." He offered a half smile with the apology. "I would like you to stay in this room with me," he said, lifting his shoulders in a shrug. "But if you prefer a room of your own, pick one."

The very fact that he didn't attempt to force the issue decided Nicole. "Oh, put the case down!" she said with feigned impatience, sweeping by him to examine the connecting bathroom.

Had she remained undecided, the sight of the bathroom would have forced her into agreeing. Like the rooms in the small foreman's house on the Sharp ranch, the spacious bathroom was an Eden of living plants. Sunlight diffused by the plastic panels in the roof-ceiling filled the room. Fitted white cabinets, which contained two shell-shaped, black-and-white marble sinks, ran the length of one wall. Along the other wall a milky-glass-enclosed shower stall separated a large bathtub from an even larger Jacuzzi. The small amount of wall space that was visible was covered by glass panels shot through with black and gold streaks. The floor was covered with deeply piled black-and-white carpet.

Feeling the warmth of J.B.'s body behind her, Nicole murmured, "How do you ever force yourself out of this room?"

J.B.'s breath tickled her ear; his soft laughter teased her senses. "Willpower," he murmured, nuzzling his face into the curve of her neck. "Wanna jump in the tub with me, honey?" he invited, tasting her warm skin with the tip of his tongue.

Gasping at the shiver that quivered through her body, Nicole closed her eyes and arched her throat to give him better access. "To bathe?" She shivered again as his arm encircled her waist.

"Whatever," he muttered, drawing her against his strength and rising heat. "We could bathe first," he whispered, splaying his hand over her taut belly. "Then shower," he murmured, cupping one breast with his gloved hand. "Then slip into the Jacuzzi." He moaned, gliding his palm to the gentle mound at the apex of her legs. "Then..." His voice trailed away as his hand caressed her through the faded denim.

Heat more intense than that generated by the Texas summer sun ran in waves through Nicole. Murmuring encouraging little sounds from deep in her throat, she slid one palm over the leather glove, the other palm over the back of his hand, and arched her body into his touch.

Her action was received by a low growl of male need and a flurry of activity. Before Nicole could draw a breath, J.B. had unsnapped her jeans and run the zipper down the short track.

"J.B.?"

"Hmmm?" he murmured distractedly, tugging gently on the tight pants. "Kick out of your sandals, honey."

Nicole obeyed without thought and a moment later stepped out of the jeans and her sheer panties. "Oh, J.B.," she moaned when his work-roughened palm smoothed the soft skin on her thigh.

"Raise your arms, love," he ordered softly, yanking her T-shirt up over her breasts.

"J.B.," she repeated, languidly lifting her arms.

"What, honey?" J.B.'s voice was warm as melted butter.

"Are we going to bathe together?" Nicole's voice was sensually low.

"That's the idea." Releasing her, he bent to pull at his boots. "If I can ever get out of these damn things."

One by one the boots came off, to arc through the air and land with a thump in one corner. His socks, jeans and briefs quickly followed.

"You forgot your shirt," Nicole whispered.

Walking around her, J.B. strode to the tub. "The shirt stays on." Turning his back, he turned on the taps, adjusting them until he had the water temperature he wanted.

"You're going to bathe with your shirt on?" Nicole squeaked in disbelief.

"The shirt stays on, Nicole." Straightening, J.B. turned to meet her wide-eyed stare. "In the tub, in the shower and in the Jacuzzi." Lifting his hand, he slowly began undoing his shirt buttons. The shirt fell apart to reveal a lean, brown, fully aroused male. "And in the bed afterward."

Nicole swallowed with difficulty. "It'll get soaked."
Nicole wasn't sure if she meant the shirt or the bed.
J.B. assumed she meant the bed.

"We won't notice, but I'll change, anyway." An
enticing smile curving his lips, he held his hand out to
her. "Come here."

Nicole could barely hear his soft voice over the
sound of gushing water, but she really didn't have to
hear him. His intent was clear in the flame that leaped
in his dark eyes. Head up, shoulders back, Nicole
crossed the floor to him, the soles of her feet tingling
from the friction of the carpet fibers beneath them. As
she drew close to J.B., the tingles crept up her legs to
dance on the sensitive inner skin of her thighs. Raw
need surged through her body when he curled his arm
around her waist and pulled her roughly against his
chest.

"God, how can I want you so badly again so
soon?" Lowering his head, J.B. sought the scar on her
shoulder with his parted lips. "I can't ever remember
wanting a woman, any woman, this much." His warm
breath moistened her skin; his words intensified the
fire licking through her veins. "Tell me you want me
as much, Nicole." His lips moved up the curve of her
neck, then nibbled at the corner of her mouth. "Tell
me you want me more than any other man."

Moaning, desperate for him, Nicole tried to capture his mouth. J.B. tormented her by holding his lips
a breath away from hers.

"Tell me, Nicole," he repeated in a harsh whisper.

"You know, J.B., you must know!" Nicole whispered. "I've never been like this with any other man."

"Never?" He wrenched a soft cry from her by out-
lining her mouth with the tip of his tongue.

"Never," she echoed, sighing as his mouth covered hers.

J.B.'s kiss was hard and possessive and wildly exciting. Sliding her arms around his taut neck, Nicole speared her fingers through his thick hair and clung, arching her body to his in blatant abandonment. The feathery glide of his hand down her spine drew a shivering response from her body. His fingers sinking gently into one rounded cheek drew a moan from deep within her throat. Water splashing over the tub's rim and onto their legs drew them apart.

"I think it's full." J.B.'s smile increased the rate of her pounding heart.

"And I'm empty."

The admission was barely out of her mouth when J.B. lifted her with one arm and swung her into the water.

"It's hot!" Nicole gasped.

"And so am I." J.B. drawled, stepping into the tub beside her. "Move over, love," he ordered softly, "and I'll scrub your front."

Nicole gave him a wry look and presented her back to him. "We'll go about this in the time-honored way," she said primly.

"You're no fun," J.B. grumbled, scooping up a sponge and a bar of soap. When her back remained squarely to him, he groaned, "Do you seriously want me to scrub your back?"

"Of course," she said, tossing her head. "And when you're finished, you can turn around for me to scrub yours."

"I'm not sure I can stand all that excitement."

"Steel yourself."

J.B. chuckled. "Honey, there *are* parts of me that are as hard as steel now."

"Never mind," she advised. "The hot water will take care of that little problem."

J.B. applied the lathered sponge vigorously to her back, then he sighed. "The hot water has made it a little problem. Whose idea was this, anyway?"

"Yours." Nicole couldn't deny a burst of laughter. "Aren't you finished with my back yet?"

"Yeah." J.B. groaned. "In fact, I think I'm finished altogether." Grasping her shoulders, he turned her to face him. "Are you ready for the shower?"

Nicole smiled at the hopeful note in his tone. "Cold, I presume?"

J.B.'s grin could only be described as evil. "And invigorating."

"But I haven't had my bath," she protested. Grabbing the sponge, she stroked it down one arm.

"Oh, hell!" J.B. exploded, working up a lather in his hands before relinquishing the soap to her. "Get on with it, then!"

Without a doubt it was the fastest bath Nicole had ever taken. The instant she set the soap and sponge aside, J.B. got up from the tub and dragged her out after him. Complaining loudly, Nicole was shoved under a stingingly cold shower spray.

"J.B., I'm freezing!" she shrieked, twisting away from both the chilling water and the cold flapping tails of his shirt.

"Yeah." J.B. grinned with satisfaction. "And I'm invigorated." Reaching for her, he drew her against his cold but reawakened body.

The strength of his kiss warmed Nicole to the point of desensitizing her to the spraying water, but not to the clammy feel of his sodden shirt. Shivering, she slipped away from him and escaped from the cubicle. She was wrapping a bath sheet around her trembling body when J.B. stepped from the shower.

"Hey," he said, whipping the towel from her numb fingers. "You're supposed to jump from the shower into the Jacuzzi."

Nicole eyed him warily. "I thought it was the other way around." Sharp suspicion edged her tone.

Obviously enjoying the entire situation, J.B. laughed and pulled her along as he walked to the large circular tub. "Come on, honey, it'll warm you up." The dripping sleeve of his shirt splattered cold water over her skin as he draped an arm around her shoulder.

"Dammit, J.B.! That shirt's got to go!" she snapped without thinking. Then she bit her lip when he went still. Raising her hand, she stroked his chest. "Josh, take it off," she murmured, coaxingly. "And not just the shirt, but the appliance, as well."

"Nicole." A hint of warning coated his voice.

"Is it all right for you to be soaking it like this?" she asked with concern.

"No."

"Then take it off," she pleaded.

"Nicole, I..." His voice trailed away, leaving an ache in her heart.

"I'll help you," she whispered.

Eight

The rays of the setting sun struck the curved side of the bubble panel on the roof, sending a shower of golden light into the room below. Bathed in the spangled glow, Nicole held her breath while J.B. silently battled with indecision. Fortunately, the inner war was brief.

The tension easing from his sharp features, J.B. moved swiftly, pulling the sodden material from his chest. When it was revealed, Nicole saw that the appliance resembled a human arm. As he lifted his right hand to unfasten the harness anchoring the artificial limb, Nicole stepped closer to him.

"Let me help you, please."

J.B. was strong, but not strong enough to withstand the compassionate understanding shining from Nicole's gold-flecked eyes. His voice low, inflectionless, he instructed her, vocally guiding her fingers. The contraption released, he eased it from his arm, then gripping it in his right hand, J.B. stood tall, magnificent in his nakedness, alert to whatever emotions crossed Nicole's expressive eyes and face.

J.B.'s muscle-corded arm ended bluntly inches below the elbow. The stump was not attractive, but it was not repulsive, either. Staring at it, Nicole was swamped by a flood of emotions so intense she swayed precariously. She'd expected to feel compassion and sadness. What she hadn't anticipated was the rage that fired her mind and emotions—rage against the stupidity and pointlessness of it all, rage against the circumstances that had inflicted damage to J.B.'s psyche infinitely more severe than to his body.

Nicole couldn't bear it, yet she knew she must. She wanted to scream to release the agony clawing at her, yet she knew she could not. Though there was nothing she could do for the man's arm, there was much she could do for the man. Gently cradling the appendage in her soft palm, she drew it carefully to her lips.

"Nicole, no." Not a shred of his former command shaded his tone; his voice was hoarse, an aching cry of protest.

But he did not physically resist. Her lips brushed the fold of skin, bestowing a whisper of a caress, then turning her head slightly, Nicole rested her cheek on the blunted arm.

"It's part of you, Josh," she murmured. "And as important as all the rest of you." Her warm tears washed the tightly drawn skin.

"Nicole." J.B.'s voice was barely audible, a mere flutter of sound in the fading gold of daylight. Dropping the man-made extension to the soft carpet, he slid his hand under her chin and lifted her head from his arm. As her gaze sought his, J.B. made no attempt to conceal the glistening brightness in his own eyes.

"You're so beautiful," he whispered. "So very beautiful."

The change in Nicole was swift and might have been daunting to a lesser man. Blinking away the tears, she raised her head and thrust out her chin defiantly. But before she could form the words of disdain she felt for the shallow compliment, J.B.'s thin lips curved into one of his slow, demoralizing smiles.

"Of course, there is one flaw in all that perfection," he drawled in his normal, rich voice.

"And that is?" Nicole arched an imperious eyebrow, positive he wasn't referring to her scarred face and shoulder.

His fabulous eyes, glistening now for an altogether different reason, slowly skimmed her long frame. When his gaze returned to tangle with hers, Nicole had the uncanny sensation she could see the devil laughing at her from the blue depths.

"You are one skinny dame."

There ensued a moment of absolute silence. Then Nicole's laughter burst like sparkling light in the room, challenging the encroaching twilight.

"You...you rangy cowpuncher!" she said with a gasp. "You muscular string bean! You have the nerve to call *me* skinny?" Tossing her head, Nicole flipped back strands of dark, dripping wet hair. "I'll have you know, my man, that I am not skinny! I am fashionably slender."

"Skinny." J.B. coiled his right arm around her waist as he made the solemn announcement. Lifting her off her feet, he deposited her still slippery wet body in the churning waters of the Jacuzzi. Retaining his hold on her, he stepped into the sunken tub, then drew her down beside him as he stretched his length in the warm silkiness of the soothing water.

"Ahhh," he sighed appreciatively, tightening his hold to draw her close to his body.

"Lovely," Nicole murmured, resting her head on his chest.

Submerged from the neck down in the bubbling water, they lay quietly for a while, savoring the aquatic massage. J.B.'s hand idly stroked her back and arm. Nicole's fingers curled into the whorls of hair on his chest.

"Is it going to pose a problem?" J.B.'s breath skipped over the top of her head.

"Is what going to pose a problem?" Nicole angled her head to test the texture of his skin with her tongue.

"Making love—" J.B.'s pause was infinitesimal "—the way I am now."

"Please don't talk like a fool." Nicole didn't even bother to raise her mouth from his chest.

"I could put the damned thing back on," he offered reasonably, moving his hand to the controls set into the broad rim around the tub.

"What for?" Nicole moved sensuously as the water temperature subtly changed from hot to warm and then to tepid.

J.B.'s hand returned to her back to stroke the delicate ridge of her spine. "I know you enjoy the sensations aroused by the glove stroking your skin." Deviltry was woven through his amused tone. "Nicole!" His tone changed abruptly when her hand slid under the water to capture a vital part of his body.

"The glove's wet," she murmured with sweet innocence while her fingers danced an ageless ritual on his tightening body.

"I—oh, Nicole!—I own a dozen leather gloves!" J.B.'s body arched responsively. Clenching his fingers into her firm bottom, he closed his eyes, so he didn't see her head dip into the water. At the sweet touch of her lips on his heated flesh, his eyes flew open. "Nicole! Sweet Lord, woman! Are you trying to drive me mad?" His voice was harsh with raw, unleashed desire.

Nicole's head broke the churning surface of the water. "Could I drive you mad, J.B.?" she asked, her lips curving into a siren's smile.

"More than likely," he muttered, again releasing her to reach for the controls on the rim of the tub. The bubbling action ceased before his hand returned to her hip. The gentle sound of water lapping the sides of the tub blended with the labored rasp of indrawn breaths.

Leaning closer to him, Nicole teased his lips with hers. "Then we have no real need of the leather, do we?" Delicately she dipped her tongue into his mouth.

"No." J.B.'s voice was little more than a groan. His fingers flexed into her satiny skin, urging her body closer to his.

Weightless in the water and eager to comply, Nicole flowed over him, around him, willingly opening to accept the fullness of him into her trembling body. Rejoicing with taking possession and being possessed, she gave voice to her joy with a shuddering moan.

Electrified, feeling stronger than ever before in his life, J.B. braced his body by clamping his left upper arm and elbow onto the tub's rim. Then he clamped

Nicole's body to his by curling his right arm around her slim hips. Fire charging through him, he heaved his hips up in a straining arc, taking, giving, conquering, surrendering.

For tension tautened minutes whispers of encouragement and whimpers of pleasure were lost in the water, churned into seething waves by a tempest of passion.

When J.B. assisted Nicole from the tub, her toes and fingertips were wrinkled, but her body was replete. Limp and pliant, she allowed him to coax her into drying his body, then stood docilely while he dried hers.

"Are you hungry?" J.B. asked, pausing in the act of rummaging through her suitcase in search of her robe.

"Mmmm," she murmured, obediently slipping her arms into the sleeves as he held the garment for her.

"I'm starving," he muttered, shrugging into a mid-thigh-length terry robe.

"Hmmm?" Nicole added a questioning inflection to her tone.

Placing his hand on her back, J.B. steered her out of the bedroom, through the mudroom and into the kitchen. "You know, honey," he said conversationally, pulling open the refrigerator door and peering into its interior, "you're a great lover, but you talk too much."

At any other time Nicole would have made a face at the mere suggestion of scrambled eggs, chunks of bacon and bits of jalapeño peppers rolled up inside a warmed flour tortilla. Yet when J.B. set a plate containing the circular sandwich and a pile of nacho chips in front of her, the delicious aroma awakened her appetite. The tall glass of icy cold beer he served with the meal went a long way toward loosening her tongue.

"How did you do that?" Indicating their empty plates, Nicole stared pointedly at J.B.'s empty sleeve.

"You'd be amazed what you can do with one hand," he replied without strain, "if you have to."

"Actually, I'm not amazed at all at what you can do with one hand." Nicole lowered her lashes to conceal the teasing gleam in her eyes. "But then I just spent two hours with you in a Jacuzzi—remember?" Her lashes swept up with feminine allure; her lips smiled with inviting sensuousness.

Sprawled lazily in the high-backed dining room chair, J.B. matched, perhaps even bested, her enticing smile. "I'm not about to forget it," he said in a pulse-stopping tone. "And we are about to repeat it." Both his tone and his smile deepened.

"J.B.! I just lost the prune look!" Nicole complained unconvincingly.

"There's always the bed," he suggested.

"We've got the supper things to clear away." Nicole sighed.

"We could clean up in the morning." J.B. arched one eyebrow.

"Race you!"

Nicole was on her feet and running before the words were completely out of her mouth. J.B. was a mere stride behind her. He caught her by the side of the king-size bed. Laughing softly, he wrapped his arm around her waist and launched them both onto the bed.

"You're a wild man," Nicole accused, wriggling free of the robe he was tugging off her.

"And you love it," he growled, nipping at her lip with his teeth.

"You're barely civilized," she charged, raking her fingernails down his taut back in response to the caressing stroke of his hand on her breast.

"And you love it," he muttered, seeking the tip of her breast with his hungry lips.

"You're insatiable," she scolded, nipping his shoulder as he slipped his hand between her thighs.

"And you love it," he groaned, entering her body with one hard move of his hips.

"Yes," she cried out with pleasure, arching into his thrust. "Yes! Yes, I love—" Nicole caught the word *you* before it escaped and changed it to "it."

Eyes closed, Nicole lay on her back, listening to the sound of her heartbeat. The thunder receded as her breathing resumed a more even, normal pattern. As it had been in the Jacuzzi, the loving had been shatteringly satisfying. Nicole's sole concern was in wondering if she'd survive.

"Come, Nicole, it's late." J.B.'s soft voice lured her sleepy gaze to his body, sprawled in utter relaxation beside her on the wide bed. "Come, sleep in my..." He hesitated, then smiled slowly. "Come sleep in my...arm."

The rays of the late-morning sun seared Nicole's naked back. She was lying facedown on a lounge chair on the patio outside the screened deck. J.B. lay prone in a similar position on a lounger close to hers. His black-gloved hand lay at rest on the small of her back, just brushing the edge of the narrow bikini girdling her hips. Comfortably aware of the weight of his hand, Nicole smiled with inner satisfaction. Though J.B.'s man-made forearm and hand was on, his shirt was off. A small victory, perhaps, she mused drowsily, but an important one.

"I'm hungry."

"You're always hungry."

"For food, woman."

"You're always hungry for that, too."

J.B. heaved a heartfelt sigh. "Are you going to cook breakfast?"

"It's almost lunchtime."

"Well, then, are you going to cook lunch?"

Now Nicole sighed, indicating harassment. "I wasn't planning on it."

"Could I talk you into changing your plans?"

"No."

"Could I bribe you into changing your plans?"

"No."

"Could I love you into changing your plans?" J.B.'s voice had lowered with each query.

"Dirty pool, Barnet." Raising her head, Nicole turned to glare at him. "Do you always get whatever you want?"

J.B.'s smile held all the appeal of a fallen angel's. "I'm hungry," he repeated. "Besides, I cooked dinner last night."

"Big deal." Pushing herself off the lounger, Nicole stood over him, clasping her loosened bikini top to her breasts. "Were you thinking of paying off before or after you eat?"

Flipping onto his back, J.B. gazed up at her while considering his answer. When he finally responded, his lips twitched to grin. "How about before *and* after?"

Nicole's chest rose enticingly with her deep sigh. "A glutton," she muttered to herself but loud enough for him to hear. "The man is an absolute glutton." She sighed again, this time wearily. "Oh, all right. If you insist."

A smile teasing her pouting mouth, she daintily dropped the skimpy bikini top onto his chest, and wiggling her fingers at him, she turned and sauntered into the house. J.B.'s roar of laughter followed her inside; J.B. was right behind the laughter.

"What did your brother mean by asking you when you were going back to work?" Nicole asked with deceptive casualness. Slowly she shifted her gaze from the lake to the man slouched in a chair next to hers. They were sitting on a dock that extended out into the lake. Though anchored to land, the end of the dock floated on buoys.

J.B. didn't look away from the fishing line he had flipped into the water. The red-and-white floater attached to the line bobbed lazily on the gentle waves. "Steve was being sarcastic." J.B.'s smile was dust dry.

Abandoning her air of indifference, Nicole persisted with open curiosity. "What was he being sarcastic about? You work for Thack." After a week of exclusive togetherness, Nicole had exhausted her repertoire of inconsequential chatter. She'd decided it was time to get to the real issues.

J.B.'s face was somber. A muscle twitched, once, in his cheek. As he stared at her, an understanding smile tilted the corners of his lips. "Playtime's over, huh?" he mused aloud.

Nicole lifted one shoulder in a half shrug. "We've had the baring of bodies, Josh."

"And now it's time for the baring of souls?"

"It was your idea," she reminded him.

"Yeah." J.B. grinned. "The baring of bodies was terrific, though, wasn't it?"

Nicole didn't grin back. She couldn't—not with the sudden sharp sense of alarm vibrating inside. "Is the baring of bodies over?" Mentally Nicole was grasping at her shredding composure; the thought of never again sharing a bed, or her body, with J.B. was intolerable.

"Don't even think it." A spasm of stark emotion swept over his face. Dropping the fishing rod, he brought his hand to her face and tenderly traced the scar with his index finger. "Don't even think it," he repeated in an intense, low tone.

Nicole's smile was tremulous. "If you'd rather, we could forgo the soul-searching."

"No." His hand fell away, leaving her cheek chilled. "Yes, I work for Thack, and Steve is well aware of it." J.B. returned to her original question abruptly. "But Steve's been riding me about going back into police work since the doctors released me with a clean bill of health," he went on to explain.

"I see." Nicole glanced away, then looked at him again. She was prepared to pursue the topic but J.B. had questions of his own.

"What about you? What are you planning to do when you go back to Philadelphia in the fall?" An odd stillness held him as he waited for her response.

"I'm not going back to Philadelphia, at least not to stay." There was a certainty to her tone that spoke of a decision firmly made.

"What do you mean you're not going back?" J.B. demanded. "Where are you going?"

"To New York." Nicole smiled. "It's past time I went back to work and stopped living off the fat of my income—so to speak."

"You're going to try modeling again?"

Nicole was shaking her head before he'd finished. "No. I have no interest in modeling anymore." Excitement tinged her tone. "I'm hoping to establish a career in finance."

"Whoa! Hold it right there!" J.B. bolted upright in the webbed deck chair. His sudden movement set the floating dock they were sitting on swaying. "Nobody ever mentioned anything about your being interested in the financial world. What sort of career? What kind of finance? What—"

"If you would kindly quiet down—" Nicole cut him off "—I'll explain."

"The floor's all yours." J.B. glanced down at the weathered boards of the dock, then grinned.

This time Nicole grinned back. "I suppose I'd better begin at the beginning," she said, frowning.

"Seems like a good place to me." Though his tone was light, his eyes were dark and narrowed, as if preparing to hear news he was positive he wasn't going to like.

"It started about six months after I went to Maine," she began pensively.

"What started?" he asked, frowning.

"The studying." Nicole glanced out over the lake. "Although the long walks I took every day tired my body, mentally I was restless." Her gaze returned to him. "Do you know what I mean?"

"Yes, I know."

Nicole nodded, musing that of course he knew. "Well," she continued, "I enrolled for night classes in a nearby community college." She laughed shortly. "I spent almost as much time driving back and forth to school as I did in class. But I stayed with it." Nicole shrugged. "I had nothing better to do."

"And you took courses in finance?" J.B. asked quietly.

"That was my original plan," Nicole replied. "But the school counselor convinced me to go for my degree. I rescheduled to day classes and graduated last fall. Along with the degree, I obtained my broker's license. Then I went home to Philadelphia."

J.B. looked astonished. "You want to be a stockbroker!"

Nicole smiled. "I *am* a stockbroker. Along the way I discovered I have a talent for the market. I've been offered an excellent position with a New York firm."

"And?" J.B.'s voice was low, tight.

"And I'm considering it. I promised them an answer by September."

J.B. was quiet for long seconds, then he asked, "What do your parents and brother think?"

"They know nothing about it." Self-mockery laced her tone. "I wanted to prove something—to them, to myself."

J.B. frowned. "Prove what?"

Nicole lifted her chin in a manner he was now familiar with, a mannerism that was challenging, defensive and heart-wrenchingly endearing.

"I wanted to prove that I am more than a beautiful face," she said fiercely. "That there is indeed intelligent life beneath the inherited bone structure and features. And I wanted to prove that by presenting them with a fait accompli." Her back stiff, Nicole stared at him, as if daring him to laugh at her personal victory.

J.B. didn't laugh; he didn't even smile. He stared at her from blue eyes glowing with admiration. Without relinquishing his visual contact, he reached down to the cooler beside his chair, withdrew a can of beer, popped the top, then held it aloft. "Well-done, Nicole," he toasted her in utter seriousness. He drank deeply, then smiled. "I only wish this was champagne, for your accomplishment deserves it."

Attired in a string bikini, seated on a plastic-webbed aluminum chair on a floating wooden dock, Nicole suddenly felt like an ermine-draped queen ensconced on a velvet-cushioned, gold-trimmed throne. And all because a one-armed man had softly said "Well-done."

The color tinting her cheeks had little to do with the relentless Texas sun. The smile on her lips had everything to do with the man sitting on a matching chair next to hers. Blinking against a rush of stinging tears, Nicole murmured, "Thank you," and lowered her gaze to the water lapping at the base of the dock.

The brilliant blue sky was clear; there were no looming thunderheads nor streaking bolts of lightning. The rocking motion came from the restless undulation of the water, not from the earth shaking beneath her feet. It was bright midday; not a single star twinkled overhead. The background sounds were of breezes ruffling the lake surface and the distant hum of a boat motor; not one note was stroked from a violin.

Quiet prevailed. Within that quiet moment Nicole realized that she'd fallen in love. Not fascination, not infatuation, but solid, forever-after love. It scared her to death.

"How do you know you have a talent for the stock market?"

Nicole was so grateful for the distraction J.B.'s question provided that she entirely missed the uneasiness woven through his tone. Raising her gaze to his, she smiled. "I dabbled a little while I was in school." Her smile faded as his expression grew skeptical. "Through my brother's management of it, the money I earned by modeling had tripled. I also have a substantial inheritance from my paternal grandfather," Nicole explained. "And though I would not risk my inheritance, I felt no compunction about speculating with the money I had earned."

"You made a profit?" J.B. asked, smiling indulgently.

Feeling that he was patronizing her, Nicole's smile narrowed. Her gaze sharpened. Her tone smoothed to silkiness. "To the tune of over half a million dollars."

"Half a million!" J.B. lost his voice.

Nicole felt satisfied. "Yes."

"And your family doesn't know?"

"No." The stiffness drained from Nicole's expression. "Not even Peter."

"And all this time they believed you were secluded in Maine licking your wounds," J.B. murmured, as if to himself. "So did Barbara." The look he gave her held more than a hint of accusation. "You allowed your family and friends to worry about you needlessly."

"That's not true, Josh!" she protested.

"No? Then what is true?" He was digging now, ruthlessly trying to understand her, yet unwilling to examine why he needed to know. "Tell me the truth about Nicole Vanzant."

Feeling pressured, cornered, Nicole exploded all over the tormentor she reluctantly loved. "The truth? Every individual has their own personal truth, don't they? I'm certainly not unique." She laughed harshly. "Except, of course, for the blessing-curse of beauty. I've been torn by conflict because of my looks since I was a child." Nicole dragged air into her body. "Have you any idea what it's like to be judged solely by your appearance? I was never quite sure whether people were drawn to me, the person, or me, the beautiful one. I'd have been a fool to hate my beauty, and I didn't. Yet at the same time I couldn't help feeling resentful because of it. I was never certain if anyone saw the woman inside the facade." Nicole swallowed, then whispered, "I was never sure if the man I thought I was in love with saw the woman behind the face."

"He hurt you?" A raw savagery edged J.B.'s voice.

"I hurt myself!" Nicole cried.

"Nicole, I don't understand."

"I didn't either for a long time." She moved her hand in a helpless manner. "J.B., I did not allow my family and friends to worry needlessly. I *was* licking my wounds in Maine. But contrary to what my family and friends believed, I was not mourning the loss of beauty. I was nursing the wounds of self-inflicted guilt."

"Guilt?" J.B. repeated, shaking his head. "About what?"

"I didn't love Jason at the time of the accident, J.B." Nicole drew a deep breath. "I never really loved him at all. I was infatuated, but never really in love." Though Nicole had resolved her inner conflict, speaking about it was even more painful and difficult than she'd imagined it would be; it was also shaming. She glanced away from him before continuing.

"I now know that I was in love with the idea of being loved—for myself. I did like Jason, though, very much," she said earnestly. "And so, to fulfill my own emotional needs, I allowed myself to drift along in the relationship, convincing myself I loved him, refusing to face his weakness and excesses." Lifting her head to meet J.B.'s steady regard was one of the most difficult things Nicole had ever had to do. Still, she did it.

"I don't like this scar." Nicole drew her finger along the faint line. "It will always remind me of my own weakness." Her hand fell to her lap. "I blamed myself for Jason's death, J.B. And I hid myself away in Maine to try to resolve my feelings of guilt."

J.B.'s eyes darkened with compassion. "Nicole, you weren't—" he began.

"I know that now," she interrupted softly. "But at the time it was very easy to accept the blame by telling myself that he would still be alive if I had been stronger, able to help him." Her smile was wry. "I realize now that there was nothing I could have done to alter circumstances. Jason had chosen his own course of self-destruction long before I ever met him. I've accepted the fact that his end was inevitable, with or without my own needs and weaknesses." A solitary tear slid down her cheek. "But I *did* indulge those needs by blinding myself to the extent of his excesses. I should not have been in that car that night and would not have been there if I hadn't been willing to believe him when he insisted that he was 'clean.'" Nicole sighed. "I console myself with the thought that maturity begins when one can accept a mistake and learn from it. Well, I learned, and I will never again seek approval of my own worth from outside influences. I found that I'm a reasonably intelligent woman with much to offer, personally and professionally. Should I ever be tempted to forget it—'' her hand again sought the mark on her face ''—all I have to do is look into a mirror. No, J.B., I was not needlessly worrying my family and friends. I was fighting for my psychological life.'' Exhausted, Nicole slumped back in her chair. He was the only person she had bared her soul to. All she could do now was love him and hope and wait for J.B.'s response.

''I want to make love with you, now, at once.'' J.B.'s voice was low, crackling with the explosive mixture of raw desire and genuine admiration. It was there, starkly defined in his tone; he wanted to make love with *her*—the woman she had revealed to him. Then another element was introduced, an element of uncertainty when he went on, ''Do you want to make love with me?''

Nicole's smile challenged the Texas sun for brilliance.

''Yes.''

Nine

Sitting cross-legged in the center of the wide bed, Nicole absently tugged her oversize T-shirt over her filmy panties and contemplated the books on the shelves opposite the bed. Her hair was tousled. Her face had a scrubbed-clean glow. Her eyebrows were drawn together as if magnetized. Her lips were set in a tight line of determination.

Tonight was the night. Nicole had made the decision while standing under the steaming shower spray. Only one full day remained of the two-week vacation. They had spent their time at the lake house lavishly—loving, laughing, talking, resting, then loving some more. They had gone out for meals twice, and both times had been memorable.

They had been at the lake for three days when J.B. suggested a break from their own cooking. On his advice Nicole had dressed in jeans and a gauzy blouse.

J.B. had worn cutoff denims and a sport shirt with the
sleeves rolled to midforearm. Nicole had considered
the concession his attire represented a compliment to
her.

The restaurant had looked like little more than a
shack from the outside and not much better inside.
The house specialty was barbecued back ribs, to be
eaten with the fingers, and it was delicious. The beer
was cold. Nicole couldn't remember the last time she'd
gotten quite so messy eating a meal or enjoyed herself
more, and she told him so. J.B. rewarded her with a
warm grin and a rather greasy kiss, right in front of
anyone who cared to watch. Nicole didn't notice if
anyone did.

It was a different story the second time they went
out. Telling her to wear something mind-shattering,
J.B. then stole her breath by looking as if he'd stepped
from the cover of a men's fashion magazine when he
stepped out of the bedroom. As they sauntered into
the dimly lit, elegantly appointed restaurant, Nicole
was amused by the conflicting emotions tugging at her.
While one part of her bristled at the lingering, ap-
praising looks sent over J.B.'s lithe body by interested
feminine eyes, another part of her unabashedly
preened with pride because he reserved his admiration for her alone. Again the food was superb, but
neatly consumed. There was no greasy kiss over the
candle-lit table; J.B. melted her bones by making love
to her with his warm, smoky-eyed glances. He reserved his kisses for later that night after they were
alone in his bedroom, and his eyes had flared with
blazing passion.

They had spent the Fourth of July holiday quietly,
stuffing their bodies with hot dogs cooked on the out-

side grill and their souls with books from his bedroom shelf. But for all the words that poured from one to the other, the flood of information about their respective childhoods, their likes and dislikes, their teenage dreams and aspirations, Nicole had been unable to successfully reopen the subject of J.B.'s work and the accident that had put an end to it.

Frustration had sparked Nicole's determination. A sense of time swiftly running out had set her decision. Eyes narrowing, she slid her gaze to the open bedroom door. She heard the distinctive pop of a champagne cork, the tinkle of glasses, then the quiet tread of his bare feet on the mudroom floor. J.B. was expecting a spectacular night.

He was humming to himself as he strolled into the bedroom. Like hers, his attire was casual—it consisted of briefs and a T-shirt. He carried two tulip-shaped glasses in his right hand. The black-gloved fingers were curled around the neck of the champagne bottle. J.B. now wore, and removed, the unconcealed appendage in front of her with easy familiarity. A slight smile softened Nicole's tight lips. Oh, yes, she mused, accepting the glass he held out to her. Tonight was definitely the night.

"Joshua Barnet, you're crazy!" Though Nicole assumed an expression of shocked indignation, she could not contain her laughter. "That's the most decadent thing I've ever heard!" Her laughter denied her outraged tone. The wine bottle was three-quarters empty, but Nicole had found no opportunity to steer the conversation along serious, soul-baring lines. The suggestion J.B. had just made concerned baring, but of her, not his soul.

"It's no more decadent than the way you react to the leather glove stroking your body," J.B. said in a reasonable tone. "Come on, love, indulge me. Take off the shirt and lie flat on the bed. I want to sip champagne from your navel." The smile he gave her incited her already rioting senses.

Nicole hesitated, then an excitement more intoxicating than the wine directed her to set aside her glass. A swift tug and her thin shirt was skimmed from her body and sent sailing across the room. She sat still for a moment, enjoying the melting sensations created inside as J.B.'s warm gaze traveled over her slender body and lingered on her small, round, jutting breasts. When his gaze rose to capture hers, she lowered herself to the bed, watching his eyes darken with passion as he leaned over her and carefully tilted the glass in his hand.

A golden drop escaped the rim and fell unerringly into the small indentation, then a second, then a third. Then, lowering his head, J.B. delicately dipped his tongue into the wine. The liquid was cold against her skin; J.B.'s tongue felt like a sizzling brand. Nicole felt a piercing fire in the heart of her femininity.

Carefully not touching her anywhere else, J.B. repeated the erotic, ritualistic performance until the glass was empty of every shimmering drop of wine and Nicole was moving restlessly against the mattress, begging him with her body to end the torment and make the ritual complete.

Setting the glass aside, J.B. tore the shirt from his torso and the briefs from his hips, then slid his wine-chilled tongue down the sensitive inner skin on her leg as he removed her panties.

"I love the sounds you make deep in your throat when you're aroused and ready for me," he murmured against the silky skin on her thigh on his return journey up her other leg. He left a string of biting little kisses from her thigh to her wine-scented navel. "You excite me to the edge of endurance when you glide like satin beneath me," he groaned, once more dipping his tongue into the enticing indentation. His right hand cupped one breast, the black leather encased its twin. "I want to act out every fantasy I ever imagined with you," he whispered, sliding his body along hers until his mouth was poised over her lips. "It might take years." He sighed, brushing his mouth over hers. "It might take forever."

Consumed by the liquid blaze coursing through her body, Nicole was beyond comprehension of his whispery words or that he had made a tentative approach to commitment. She was on fire, a living torch, burning only for him. Enclosing him within a lover's embrace, she welcomed him joyously into her body and gave herself completely. Striving to give him pleasure, Nicole attained her own ecstasy.

Tonight was the night.

The intrusive thought nagged at the contented haze luring Nicole's consciousness toward the edge of slumber. She moved restlessly in a futile attempt to flick the thought aside. She was deliciously comfortable. Her body felt sweetly drained. J.B.'s arm was strong.

Tonight was *supposed* to be the night.

Nicole frowned at the persistent thought. She didn't want to think; she wanted to sleep. Tomorrow, she promised herself; she'd talk to J.B. tomorrow. Curl-

ing closer to the warmth of his body, Nicole blanked
her mind of all disruptive thought and slowly drifted
off to sleep.

The mingled aromas of fresh coffee and hot cinnamon rolls teased Nicole from dreamless unconscious-
ness. Inhaling deeply, she turned onto her back and
opened her eyes. J.B. was seated in the easy chair by
the rectangular window that ran almost the entire
length of the side wall. On the table beside the chair
was a pot of coffee, a container of milk, two squat, fat
mugs and a plate with the steaming breakfast rolls.
The window behind the table was streaked with rivu-
lets of rain. Beyond the window the lake water
thrashed wildly. Jagged fingers of lightning speared
the roiling clouds overhead.

"It's raining!" Having made the profound excla-
mation, Nicole frowned and glanced around for her
robe.

"I know." Aware and amused by her modesty in the
morning, regardless of how wildly uninhibited she
might have been the night before, J.B. stood and
turned his back to pour the coffee. "It's at the foot of
the bed," he murmured, referring to the garment she
was searching for.

He was staring through the rain-splattered window,
sipping his coffee as Nicole dashed into the bathroom. He was seated in the chair again when she returned moments later, face washed, teeth cleaned and
hair brushed. The smile playing on his lips brought a
flush to her scrubbed cheeks. Averting her eyes from
the devilish gleam in his gaze, Nicole dropped into the
matching chair on the other side of the table.

"Coffee?" J.B. asked politely, forcing her to look
at him.

"Yes." Nicole ran a quick, appreciative glance over him as she accepted the mug he held out to her. The swim trunks and cutoff denims that he had worn exclusively since their arrival at the lake had been exchanged for jeans that clung to his narrow hips and muscular flanks. The Texas Lone Star flag was emblazoned on the blue sweatshirt he had pulled on against the damp chill. His feet were once again encased in boots. To Nicole he looked more appetizing than the iced cinnamon rolls. Tempted to taste, she smiled but reached for a roll instead. Sinking her teeth into the warm, spicy dough, she envisioned a supple, muscular shoulder.

"What are you thinking about?" J.B. asked, studying the heightened color in her cheeks.

"You," she replied, grinning at him. "I was comparing you to this bun." She waved the confection, then bit off another piece.

"You think I'm as soft as a rolled pastry?" J.B. arched his dark eyebrows and scowled.

"Uh-uh." Nicole shook her head, then swallowed before elaborating. "Quite the contrary. I believe you're very much the tough hombre Barbara said you were."

"Barbara said I was tough, did she?" Amusement threaded J.B.'s low tone.

"Yes." Nicole popped the last bit of roll into her mouth, then licked melted icing off her finger.

"She was right, I am." Leaning back in the chair, he smiled benignly. "I seduce skinny ex-model stockbrokers without a twinge of conscience." His smile turned predatory. "So what do you want to do today? Play chess? Listen to some music? Read? Be seduced?"

"I've been," Nicole retorted, faking a yawn. Then, remembering what she'd promised herself, she grew serious. "What I'd like to do is have a few questions answered."

Now J.B. faked a yawn that didn't quite conceal his sudden tension. "I've been answering questions for two weeks. Are you really a stockbroker or a secret agent for the FBI?" Before she could respond, he went on, "I've just about told you my life history, down to the fact that I prefer rare steak, the color blue, ice-cold beer, sleeping in the raw and—" he flashed a wicked grin "—lacy teddies. What else could you possibly want to know?" he concluded, the grin fading.

Undaunted, Nicole smiled. "Well, for one thing, I'm curious about what your father meant when he said this house is yours while you keep referring to it as your father's."

J.B. skimmed a glance around the large room. Then he sighed. "This house *is* my father's. It will belong to me after his death."

"You will inherit it?" Nicole frowned, thinking about his brother. When he nodded, she put the thought into words. "But what about Steve? Surely he—"

"Steve gets the ranch." J.B.'s tone was brisk.

"But—"

"Let me explain the situation before you object." J.B. raised a hand to silence her. "My father loves that ranch. All Austin has ever wanted was to ride his horse on his own land." His smile was dry. "Ten years ago a major oil company leased drilling rights from Dad. The royalty payments from the oil pumped from his land have made him a millionaire several times over." He acknowledged Nicole's gasp with a smile and a nod. "Dad built this place the first year after the money started rolling in, and when he discussed the terms of the new will he was having drawn up, I assured him I'd be more than happy to have this house instead of a half interest in the ranch. Steve has worked his tail off on that place because, like Dad, he loves it. Steve has earned every inch of the land, whereas it's just another ranch to me."

"And the money?" Nicole's voice revealed the awe she felt.

"Oh, Steve and I will probably share that." His shrug was careless, dismissive. "I'd just as soon Mother and Dad spent every dollar of it enjoying themselves, but they won't." J.B. lifted one eyebrow. "Any other questions?"

Nicole stared at him for a moment. She didn't doubt the sincerity of his disclaimer; it was obvious that J.B. simply didn't care about the millions of dollars the Texas black gold had poured into his father's bank account. But J.B. did care, and deeply, about something else. And that was what Nicole needed answers about. "Yes," she finally replied. "Like Steve, I can't help but wonder when you're going to go back to work." Chilled by his hardening expression, Nicole had to fight an urge to bolt from the chair.

"I work for Thack." J.B.'s tone was cold, his eyes remote.

Intimidated but determined, Nicole strove for a cool tone; she almost achieved it. "But ranching isn't what you really want to do for the rest of your life, is it?"

"Drop it, Nicole." J.B.'s beautiful eyes glittered with warning. In that instant Nicole could see how very much of a tough hombre he could be. "One-armed cops are useless on the streets of a city."

J.B.'s attitude had a strange effect on Nicole. Sharp anger seared through her. Raising her chin, she met his cold-eyed stare with blazing defiance. "Drop it?" she repeated. "How dare you say that to me? Have you conveniently forgotten your own suggestion of soul-baring here?"

"Nicole—"

"Nicole, nothing!" She cut him off angrily. "Damn you, J.B., I told you everything about myself!" Springing up, Nicole glared down at him. "And now you have the gall to tell me to *drop* it! Well, I won't drop anything! I gave you answers. Now I want some in return."

Gazing up at her slim, challenging form, J.B. surrendered to the warmth stealing through him. "Are you going to hit me?" His tone was serious, but his eyes gleamed.

"I'm considering it."

"Reconsider." J.B. smiled and motioned at the chair. "Sit down, please." His sigh signaled defeat. "What do you want to know?"

Sinking into the chair, Nicole leaned forward to gaze at him intently. "Barbara said you were offered a promotion after the accident and that you turned it down. Is that correct?" J.B. nodded. "But why?" Nicole cried. "You'd have still been doing police work!"

"From behind a desk?" J.B. sneered. "Let me explain something to you. Anglo-Celt blood flows through my veins. I'm a direct descendant of the border Scots who opened the way west, the frontiersmen who blazed the trails from the east, mostly your own Pennsylvania, through the Appalachians and the Cumberland Gap. My ancestors were with Houston at

San Jacinto." His features were haughty with fierce pride. "The border Scots, or Scots-Irish, or whatever historians call them, were warriors. Their fighting worth was proved at both the Alamo and San Jacinto. I am one of the warriors. My frontier is crime. I'm a street cop. What in hell would I do stuck behind a desk, even if that desk was in an office with my name printed on the door?" His stare now challenged her.

Nicole accepted the challenge by tossing it right back at him. "Fight crime from a different position?"

"You don't understand." J.B.'s voice was harsh.

"Maybe I understand too well," Nicole retaliated. "I can understand that working behind a desk would play hell with your self-image of the defender on the wall or by the edge of the swamp." She smiled bleakly when he stiffened. "I do know some Texas history, Josh, and I believe you'd serve Texas as well from behind a desk as those defenders did on the walls of the Alamo and at the edge of the swamp at San Jacinto."

"My image?" J.B.'s voice was cold, his eyes were even colder. His right hand gripped the arm of the chair. A muscle twitched in his lean cheek. He wasn't angry; J.B. was rigid with fury. "What the hell do you think I am, some posturing prima donna?"

Nicole didn't believe J.B. would hurt her, yet the depth of his anger frightened her. The muscles over her stomach clenching, she pressed her back into the chair. "I didn't say that, Josh." Her tone was soft, soothing. "I never even thought it."

"Of course you thought it!" J.B. sprang from the chair. "My image?" He shook his head, as if confused. "Two weeks! We've been together for two solid weeks, and you don't know me at all!" Raking his hand through his hair, he turned and strode across the room. When he turned to face her again, his features were set in unrelenting lines. "All this time you believed I was playing champion of the people out there on the streets, didn't you?" Nicole opened her mouth to protest; he wouldn't allow it. "You've as much as accused me of feeding my ego on the past. Well, let me tell you a few hard facts, lady." His steps slow, J.B. walked toward her. "There are some very nasty folks out there on the street. They steal and hook kids on drugs and kill. The one thing they don't do is play games." Coming to a stop, he loomed over her. "Do I see myself as a champion of the people? You're damned right I do, and I wasn't playing at it."

"Josh, please." Nicole's throat ached, her heart ached more.

"I was a good cop, Ms. Stockbroker Vanzant." J.B.'s sharp tone sliced into her soul. "I never hustled anyone. I was never on the take. I earned my pay." His gaze dropped to the black-gloved hand. A tired smile moved his lips. "If it was all playacting, I gave too damned much of myself to the performance of my *role*."

Nicole wanted to defend herself, but she wanted to defend him more. "It was not a gesture, Josh," she said. "You've earned the promotion." She raised her hand to touch him and bit hard on her lip to subdue a cry of pain when he stepped back.

"I'm a street cop." J.B. enunciated each word. "And if I can't perform on the street, I'll play home on the range as Thack's foreman."

"While your soul writhes in agony," Nicole murmured.

"It's my soul."

"Yes." Nicole sighed in defeat. He was so very close, and so very far away. "Yes." Shoulders drooping, she glanced from the hard glitter of his eyes to the rain-streaked window. The vacation was over; the lake had lost its charm. "I want to leave here today." Nicole didn't look at him; she couldn't.

"Why?" J.B.'s voice was low and hard. "Have you decided you don't like me anymore?" he asked with cool mockery.

"Like you!" Nicole turned to gaze up at him, her eyes dark with despair. "Josh, you terrify me!"

He reacted as if she'd struck him. "Nicole! I'd never harm you!"

"You don't understand." Nicole shook her head. "Josh, I'm not afraid of you, at least not in the physical sense. But I have just managed to resolve my own emotional problems. I'm not up to dealing with yours."

"I haven't asked you to," J.B. retorted. "Have I?"

"No, you haven't asked me to." Nicole's smile was sad. "But, you see, worry and concern go hand in hand with love, and I'm very much afraid I'm falling in love with you."

Love.

The word resounded inside J.B.'s head. *Love. Damn! Who needs it?*

J.B. kept his narrowed gaze on the rain-slick road, refusing to look at the woman who had introduced the word into the discussion several hours previously. Deliberately withdrawing into himself, he had denied himself the pleasure of looking at her. J.B. knew that if he looked at Nicole, he'd want to touch her, and touching her was out of the question. He had to think and, he hoped, sort out his tangled emotions.

A road sign indicated a sharp curve ahead. J.B. eased his booted foot from the accelerator. A wet road was not conducive to in-depth thought. They were over halfway back to the Sharp ranch. Contemplation, speculation, introspection would have to wait. J.B. needed to be alone, away from the distracting influence of the woman who was *afraid* she was falling in love with him.

Love. Damn! A tight feeling invaded J.B.'s chest. At that moment he was very much afraid he *needed* love. It scared the hell out of him.

"Nicole, you look awful!" Barbara stood just inside the door to Nicole's room, her eyes wide with concern. "What in the world happened between you and J.B.?"

Nicole forced a smile as she glanced up from the open suitcase on her bed. "Everything," she said, her smile faltering. "Everything and nothing."

"That doesn't make sense!" Barbara moved to the end of the bed. "What does everything and nothing mean?"

The shirt she was holding fell unnoticed from Nicole's hand. Heaving a sigh, she sank onto the edge of the bed. "It means that being with J.B. was everything I ever dreamed being with a man could be." She blinked against a rush of tears to her eyes. "And it means that nothing constructive came of it." Her shrug was not convincing. "Everything and nothing."

Skirting around the foot of the bed, Barbara shoved the case aside and sat down next to Nicole. "And what about J.B.?"

Nicole's attempt at a laugh was even less convincing than her shrug. "J.B.?" she said, giving a half shake of her head. "What can I say? How do I begin to figure out a man like J.B.?"

"There's more to the man than you originally thought?" Barbara's smile conveyed sad amusement.

"You know there is." Nicole smiled back in understanding. "What can one say about a man who is tough, really tough, but who is capable of gentleness and tenderness, as well? How does one figure a man who reads everything from Kipling to King and enjoys listening to music ranging from Bach to the Boss?" Nicole lifted her hands in a helpless gesture. "Barbara, the man fills his private space with all kinds of living plants!"

"That's bad?"

"It's baffling!" Jumping up, Nicole strode to the window. "He loves his family. He genuinely likes most people." She turned slowly. "J.B.'s intelligent, he's fun to be with, he's a good person. But he has this *thing* about being a street cop. He's tearing himself apart from the inside out!" she cried. "And I can't help him."

"You're in love with him."

"Yes, I'm in love with him." Returning to the bed, Nicole sat down heavily. "And I think I should run for my life."

"J.B. doesn't love you?" Barbara grasped Nicole's trembling fingers, as if knowing the answer.

Nicole clung to her friend's hand. "No, J.B. does not love me." She glanced away. "Oh, I suppose he likes me well enough, but J.B. won't allow himself to love any one woman. Loving a woman just might take his mind off the bitterness eating at his soul."

"Nicole!" Barbara's fingers tightened spasmodically around Nicole's. "That's unfair."

"What J.B. is doing to himself is unfair," Nicole retorted. "He's going through the motions of life, Barbara. I know, I've been there. And unless he resolves his inner turmoil, he'll wind up a very bitter man."

Barbara bit her lip, then sighed. "Thack has tried to talk to him, several times. J.B. deliberately changes the subject. How can we help him, Nicole?"

"We can't." Nicole looked utterly helpless. "J.B. must work his own way out of pain and regret and loss. It isn't easy." She closed her eyes. "Coming to terms with a shattered life is very, very difficult." Opening her eyes again, Nicole managed a weak smile. "I know, I've been there."

"Oh, Nicole, I'm so sorry!" Barbara was quiet for a moment, then she asked, "What are you going to do?"

"I don't know." The expression on Nicole's pale face was stark. "I want to run, put half a continent between us. I keep telling myself that if I weren't here, couldn't see him, I'd soon forget. And yet I know it's not true. Whether I'm near him or not, whether I see him or not, I won't forget." The eyes she raised to Barbara were dark with despair. "I love him. I didn't want to, but I do. Nothing's going to change the way I feel. I might as well stay."

Ten

You got a burr under your saddle, friend?'' A thread of concern ran through Thack's sardonic tone. ''You've been a mite edgy the past two weeks.''

Two weeks? Had it only been two weeks since he and Nicole had returned from the lake? It seemed more like two months to J.B. His expression wry, J.B. straightened away from the fence he'd been repairing. Raising his good arm, he tilted his straw hat to the back of his head and wiped the sweat from his brow onto the sleeve of his cotton shirt. As he lowered his arm, he slanted a narrow-eyed glance at Thack. ''It's hot.''

''It usually is in July, but the heat's never made you surly before,'' Thack retorted, dismissing J.B.'s explanation as inadequate. ''You've never before come back from a vacation looking like you'd been trampled by a herd of buffalo, either.'' Thack grimaced.

"What in hell went wrong between you and Nicole, anyway?"

"Back off, Thack." J.B.'s voice was low with warning.

"Back off, Thack?" Thack repeated, too softly. "Back...off...Thack?" His brown eyes darkened to near black as he stared at J.B. "No." Thack shook his head once, sharply. "I damn well won't back off." Drawing himself up to his full height of six feet four inches, he leveled a cool gaze on J.B. "We need to powwow, friend." Turning abruptly, Thack strode to the truck parked near the fence. "Come have a beer."

"No, thanks." J.B.'s cool tone was belied by the coiled look of readiness that radiated from him.

Whirling, Thack gave J.B. a predatory smile. "That wasn't an invitation," he murmured. "That was a direct order."

"Thack—"

"Dammit, Josh! I said come have a beer!" Thack cut J.B. off impatiently. "I want to talk—now!"

J.B. remained still for a moment. Then his lips tilted in a dangerous smile. His shoulders rippled in a slight shrug. His movements economical, he pried the gloved fingers from around the handle of the wire cutters he'd been using. Then, taking his time, he ambled to the side of the truck and nodded his thanks for the can of cold beer Thack offered him.

"Okay, boss, what's on your mind?" J.B. lifted the can in salute before downing half the contents in a few deep swallows.

With the litheness of a much smaller man, Thack eased down to hunker on the heels of his boots. "Have a seat and I'll tell you." He gestured to the dusty ground around him.

J.B.'s lips tightened, but he crossed his ankles and lowered himself into a cross-legged sitting position. "Let's have it."

"You look like hell," Thack said bluntly. When J.B. made no response, he continued, "Nicole looks even worse." This time Thack got a reaction; J.B. flinched. "Look, Josh, we've been friends a long time, and you know me well enough to know I don't stomp around on anyone's business." The rough edges had smoothed from Thack's tone. He was quiet until J.B. gave a brief nod. "This is different. This is my turf. Nicole is a guest in my home. And I've had it with watching the two of you. Dammit, J.B., you look like a thunder-cloud, and she looks like a ghost!"

J.B. felt the verbal jab clear through to the pit of his gut. The reaction jerked his head up. "What do you mean, she looks like a ghost?" His voice was hoarse, uneven.

Thack expelled his breath harshly. "Haven't you looked at her, man? She's pale. She's lost weight. There are dark circles under her eyes." Thack's fingers gripped the beer can. "And she's so damned quiet. What the hell did you do to her?"

J.B. held Thack's accusing stare for a moment, then he glanced down. "I didn't do anything to Nicole." His voice was low, tired. "We had a difference of opinion, that's all."

"What about?"

J.B.'s head snapped up. "None of your damned—"

"Don't give me that!" Thack again cut him off. "Nicole looks like walking death, and Barbara doesn't look much better. You can hide out in your own place. I'm the one who has to watch those two women, and

I don't mind telling you that it's driving me nuts."
Thack tossed the empty can into the truck bed with
unnecessary force. "So let's hear it, buddy. I want to
see my woman smiling again. Nicole, too."

J.B. hesitated for long seconds, then he sighed in
defeat. In an unemotional tone he gave Thack a brief,
glossed-over account of the two weeks he'd spent with
Nicole at the lake house, finishing his narrative with
their final argument. "She as much as accused me of
using my work on the police force to feed my overin-
flated ego." He shrugged. "Hell, maybe she's right."

"Knock it off." Thack's voice was tight. "You and
I both know that you were never that kind of cop."
Pulling his hat from his head, he raked his fingers
through his blond waves. "I do agree with Nicole
about one thing, though."

J.B. eyed Thack warily. "And that is?" He knew
the answer, and still he'd had to ask.

"You're playing at this." He indicated the surrounding area with a sharp wave of one hand. "You
want to ranch about as much as I want to hang naked
by my heels in downtown Fort Worth."

J.B.'s lips twitched. "Conjures up an interesting
picture, though," he said, fighting the first urge he'd
had to smile in two weeks.

"Don't change the subject." Thack flashed a grin
that quickly faded. "J.B., I know I promised you a
long time ago that I'd never mention this again, but
dammit, friend, you're killing yourself inside by staying away from the work you love."

J.B.'s features began to lock, but before he could
growl a protest, Thack went on in a low, earnest tone.

"Look, Josh, I understand how you feel, I always
have. But you're wrong in believing that the promo-

tion was offered because you lost your arm in the line of duty." J.B. opened his mouth. Thack silenced him by slicing his hand through the air. "I know you were the best on the street, but Josh, the physical work was only the icing on the police force cake. It was your mind that made you the best, not your muscle. There wasn't another man on the force who could equal your investigative work. And that's why they renew the offer at regular intervals. They need you, J.B. It's as simple as that."

His features frozen, his eyes cold, J.B. sat unmoving on the dusty ground and stared long and hard at the friend he would have laid his life on the line for without an instant's hesitation. Hunched down, ignoring the sweat collecting on his forehead around the edge of his hat, Thack stared back—and held his breath.

"I'll think about it."

The pent-up breath eased from Thack's chest. J.B.'s concession wasn't great, but it was a step in the right direction. Having tested the bonds of friendship that far, Thack shrugged and decided to keep going. "And Nicole? Will you think about her, too?"

"You're pushing it, Thackery."

"I'm a brave man." Thack grinned as the tautness in his muscles eased; J.B. only called him Thackery when he was teasing. "So will you think about her?"

"Oh, hell, Thack!" One flowing movement and J.B. was upright, staring down at his boss. "I haven't thought about anything but Nicole in two weeks." His lips curved in a derisive smile as he returned to the fence. Hadn't his preoccupation with Nicole been the reason for making a phone call to Fort Worth that very morning—even though he hadn't decided yet if he would actually keep the appointment?

Nicole was standing on the shaded porch when J.B. drove the truck into the ranch yard. Squinting through the plume of dust billowing into the air from the vehicle's passage, she strained to catch a glimpse of the stern man behind the wheel. A soft sigh whispered through her lips as the truck disappeared from sight around the side of the house.

J.B. had been avoiding her ever since their return from the lake house. He had not been to the main house for a meal during those endless two weeks. On the occasions he had come to confer with Thack, he had been polite and withdrawn. After the second such meeting Nicole had made herself scarce when she saw that he was on his way to the house. After two weeks of wanting him through long days and longer nights, Nicole was starving for the sight of him.

Trailing her fingers along the warm metal railing, Nicole strolled to the end of the porch to glance with apparent uninterest toward the ranch foreman's quarters. Her breath caught on a deeper sigh as she saw J.B. step from the truck and slam the door. Her gaze intent, full of longing, she watched him open the gate. When he turned to close it again, he glanced up, as if knowing she was there. For an eternity of seconds they stared at each other across the short distance of the yard. Then he turned and walked to his front door.

Nicole didn't see J.B. enter the house. Telling herself the glare from the sun caused the sting in her eyes, she closed them.

"Hi."

Nicole shivered from the warmth in J.B.'s low-pitched voice. She blinked, then raised her hand to shade her eyes and conceal the brightness in them. "Hi." Never had one tiny word been harder to articulate.

His feet planted slightly apart in the well-tended grass around the house, J.B. stood gazing up at her, his eyes shaded by the wide brim of his straw hat, his lips curved into a beguiling smile. "Still mad at me?"

"I never was mad at you, Josh." Nicole ran her tongue over her dry lips and swallowed a moan when his gaze dropped to her mouth. "I...I know I have no right to tell you any—"

"You have the right," he interrupted in a rough whisper. "The time we spent together gave you that right." J.B. stood still, waiting, and when she didn't respond, he sighed. "I miss you," he said, caressing her with a glance. "I miss laughing with you, cooking with you, being quiet with you." His voice roughened even more. "I miss loving with you."

"Josh!" It was a soft, anguished cry from her heart.

J.B. closed his eyes as a tremor ran the length of his body. "I'm leaving tomorrow." If he had wanted to get a reaction from her, J.B.'s hopes were satisfactorily fulfilled.

"Leaving?" Nicole exclaimed. "But why? Where are you going?" She ignored the fact that his actions were none of her business; as far as Nicole was concerned, everything about Joshua Barnet was now her business.

A smile softened the tight line of his thin lips. "I have an appointment with my former boss, Captain Stankawitz, in Fort Worth."

The wrought-iron rail dug into Nicole's soft palms. "J.B., that's wonderful!" She gripped the rail more tightly to control her trembling excitement.

"I'm not making any promises," J.B. warned, reaching up to cover her fingers with his hand. "I agreed to talk to the man, that's all."

"But it's a start!" Nicole cried. "J.B., it's an enormous step in the right direction!"

"Maybe. We'll see." Removing his hand, J.B. stepped back. "But remember, I said no promises." He repeated his warning.

Nicole smiled. "I'll remember." She watched him turn away, then called after him, "J.B., why don't you come over for dinner? Ellie's been grumbling about missing your sassy mouth at the table."

J.B. tossed her a grin over his shoulder. "Not tonight. I plan to get an early start. But you tell Ellie that I'll be wanting to talk to her about sass over the supper table the night I get back."

He was moving away, and Nicole had to raise her voice to be heard. "And when will that be?"

"I'm not sure," he called back. "Couple of days, maybe more."

"Josh!" Nicole yelled. "Why are you in so much of a hurry?"

J.B. stopped short and turned slowly to look back at her. "Why? Because I want to kiss you so damned much I can hardly stand it, that's why. And if I kiss you, it won't stop there, and I'll never get the hell to Fort Worth!" Swinging around, he kicked up dust as he strode across the yard.

Her eyes misty with reborn dreams, her smile soft, her steps light, Nicole drifted along the porch to the door. It was after she'd walked inside that the destructive thought shattered her euphoria. J.B. wanted her!

Eyes widening, Nicole shook her head. No. Wanting her was the wrong reason. She didn't want him going to Fort Worth for her! She had to stop him. When, and if, J.B. was ready to resolve the problems he'd been left with after the accident, it had to be for *him*!

As soon as dinner was over and the dining room and kitchen restored to order, Nicole went to the nursery to talk to Barbara.

"I can't let him do it," Nicole said decisively after telling Barbara about J.B.'s plans and her own feelings on the matter.

"How can you stop him?" Barbara murmured, gently rocking Rita.

Nicole sighed. "I don't know, but I must try." She moved to the door. "I'm going over to his house." Her smile was both hopeful and sad. "Don't wait up."

"Good luck."

I'll probably need more than luck, Nicole thought, crossing the yard to J.B.'s house. At the door she hesitated for a moment, then she knocked firmly. She rushed into speech the instant he opened the door.

"I must talk to you, Josh. May I come in?" The question was academic; she stepped inside even as she asked it.

Obviously surprised, J.B. took a step back, then immediately stepped forward again. Reaching past Nicole, he pushed the door shut. As he brought his arm back, he caught her around the shoulders and pulled her to him.

"Josh!"

Nicole's voice and breath were trapped inside J.B.'s hungry mouth. His arm tightening compulsively, he pulled her close to him while his parted lips moved with slow deliberation on hers.

Nicole had not come to him for an embrace. She'd come to talk, argue, even fight with him if necessary, to make him understand that he mustn't base the biggest decision of his life on her.

Nicole didn't fight, she didn't argue, she didn't even talk. Moaning deep in her throat, she curled her arms around his taut neck and returned his kiss with fervent desire.

Their tongues dueled and stroked and filled each other in turn, making silent demands, giving unspoken answers. J.B.'s hand splayed at the base of her spine, fingers sinking urgently into her softly rounded flesh. Nicole's nails raked his shoulders, relaying the urgency back to him.

They didn't make it to the bedroom; they barely made it to the couch. Articles of clothing were swiftly removed and carelessly flung aside. Words were unnecessary. Breathing was labored and harsh. A low growl vibrated in J.B.'s throat as he cast off the last remnant of civilization. His mouth crushed her lips as his body joined hers in the most basic celebration of life.

The tension spiral was immediate and could not endure. The flames were all-consuming. Ecstasy was swiftly attained. Their gasped cries of completion blended in a simultaneous, primitive sound of exquisite repletion.

Silence and sanity were restored. The sensual heights were lost to the intrusion of reality. Reality was not without humor.

"You were right." Brushing a final kiss over his cheek, Nicole pushed lightly against J.B.'s shoulders.

"About what?" Capturing her mouth one last time, J.B. then slid off the couch to sit on the floor. Too relaxed to sit up, Nicole stretched out beside him on the floor.

Her lips curved teasingly. "You definitely are a warrior."

J.B. looked startled by the compliment, then the rich, vibrant sound of his laughter chased the shadows from the room—and Nicole's mind. The gold flecks in her dark eyes glowing with contentment, she raised her hand to trail her fingertips down his naked arm to the gloved hand.

"Why have you suddenly decided to go to Fort Worth?"

"Because I love you." J.B.'s voice was low; his beautiful blue eyes were soft.

Nicole wanted to laugh with joy—and sob in despair. Instead, she carefully twined her fingers around the inanimate digits encased in leather. "That's the wrong reason, Josh." Her voice was steady.

"No, love, it's the right reason." Smiling, J.B. lifted his hand and brushed his fingers over her cheek. "Trust me, my skinny darling," he urged, his smile growing as her eyes flashed. "I said I'll make no promises in regard to this meeting tomorrow, and I won't. But trust me until I get back. Okay?"

"Okay," Nicole murmured as his hand fell away. "But if you call me skinny again, you just might not live to ever see Fort Worth."

"Now who's the warrior?" Springing to his feet, J.B. drew her up beside him. His right hand traced the curves of her left side. "You've lost weight." His tone was grim.

Arching one eyebrow, Nicole stepped back to run a glance over his honed figure. "So have you."

"I missed you." J.B. smiled derisively. "I couldn't eat."

"Neither could I."

"I couldn't sleep too well, either." Self-mockery colored his tone.

"Neither could I."

J.B.'s smile sent a shiver dancing along Nicole's spine.

"Let's go to bed."

Thack received the disturbing phone call early in the morning on the third day of J.B.'s absence. He was frowning when he returned to the breakfast table.

"Who was it, darling?" Barbara's frown mirrored her husband's.

"An informer." Thack smiled wryly into the faces of the three shocked women. "A contact from my Ranger days."

"But what did he want with you?" Barbara asked, her frown deepening.

"Money." Thack grimaced.

Barbara's eyes grew round. "But why would he think you'd give him money?"

Thack's wide shoulders rippled with a shrug. "He thought I'd reward him out of gratitude."

"For what?" Barbara cried in exasperation. "Thackery, will you please explain!"

"Don't blow a gasket, honey." Thack's tone soothed. "The guy told me a cock-and-bull story about drug drops being made here on my property."

"Here!" Barbara exclaimed.

"Honey, I asked you *not* to blow a gasket." Thack shot a warning look at the other two members of his audience. "The guy's broke. He's looking for a patsy. Hell, maybe he thinks my brain turned to mush when I retired. I don't know."

"But what did he say?" Barbara insisted.

"He claims the deals have been going down at that old line shack in the hills for some time now but that he only heard about it earlier this morning." Thack's lips twisted wryly. "He said that the story he picked up was that with both J.B. and me on the property, and with our reputations as law officers, the runners feel safe enough to make the drops in broad daylight."

"Could there be any truth to the man's story, Thack?" Nicole spoke for the first time since Thack had reentered the room.

"I seriously doubt it." Thack looked more amused than concerned. "But I'll check it out—" he grinned "—just to keep the nervous one here happy."

"You won't go alone?" Ellie said sharply.

"No, I'll pull my men away from their work," Thack retorted sarcastically. "Come on, Ellie. The guy probably spent the night curled up with a bottle of cheap wine—which is now empty. He needs money for another bottle, and he decided to try shaking me down. *I'll* have a look around the old shack myself. I'm sure as hell not going to have my men waste the day because of some alcohol-induced fairy tale."

Thack's tone was so confident it sent a shiver of apprehension through Nicole. Keeping her suspicions to herself, Nicole finished her meal, then helped with the cleaning up. But the moment the work was done, she excused herself to Barbara for the remainder of the day by telling her she was going to clean J.B.'s house.

Concealed behind the lacy curtain at the window in J.B.'s living room, Nicole watched Thack saddle his horse and ride out of the ranch yard. Astride a gentle mare, she followed him fifteen minutes later. Nicole knew where she was going and how to get there; Barbara had shown her the shack during a tour of the property the week before.

Allowing the mare to daintily pick her own way over the rough, hilly terrain, Nicole pondered the wisdom of her action. "I'm probably way off base, you know," she told the horse in a conversational tone. The mare's ears twitched in response. "But I did have that weird dream the day I arrived here," she mused, frowning. The mare snorted loudly.

Nicole laughed and silently agreed with the animal. There wasn't the least similarity between her present position and the odd dream she'd had that first afternoon at the ranch. She was not on foot. It wasn't dark or cold. She felt no sense of a menacing presence—male or otherwise.

Nicole laughed again, then stopped abruptly as a disquieting thought occurred to her. Thack *could* be in danger. She urged the mare into a faster pace as another memory came to mind. The memory was of Barbara's voice the day they had toured the ranch. They had been laughing about Barbara's account of Thack's apparent tendency to be accident-prone.

"He told me once that he actually backed off a roof while helping a friend repair it," Barbara had related with a grin.

But what persisted in haunting Nicole was the sudden change in Barbara's expression and voice and her words when she starkly confessed, "I pray for him every time he's out of my sight, Nicole, because I'd die if anything ever happened to Thack."

Loving J.B. the way she did, Nicole understood and shared Barbara's concern. Foolish errand or not, Nicole determinedly continued toward the unused line shack.

She got her first look at the nearly collapsed, one-room building as the mare crested a steep incline. Gasping aloud, Nicole brought the horse to a halt with a sharp tug on the reins. An alarm sounded shrilly in her mind at the sight of two four-wheel-drive vehicles parked in the scant shade thrown by the weathered shack. There was no sign of Thack or his horse.

What to do? Indecision held Nicole motionless for a moment. Then, before she could change her mind, she slid from the mare and tied the reins to a low, prickly bush. Moving cautiously and as quietly as possible in her heeled boots, Nicole approached the side of the cabin.

There was one window, cracked and filthy with years of accumulated grime. Circling the vehicles, she crept to the corner of the window. Nicole heard a low whinny and the rattling sound of hooves moving restlessly on the rocky ground at the same instant she stole a peek through the dirty pane. Biting back a gasp, she pulled away and flattened herself against the rough boarded building.

Perspiration beaded her forehead and slicked her palms. Her breathing was strained and uneven. Neither condition had anything to do with the July heat. Closing her eyes, Nicole had a mental image of the scene she'd caught a glimpse of. The door to the shack was hanging open. A long, rectangular patch of sunlight illuminated the filthy floorboards of the interior. Hands clasped at the back of his head, Thack stood inside the doorway, his body casting a long shadow in that patch of golden light. But the sight of the two men facing Thack was what had drawn the color from Nicole's face.

The men were attired in business suits. Their white shirts gleamed in the shadows beyond the splash of sunlight. Their neckties were subdued and conservative. The only jarring note in their otherwise normal appearance were the nasty-looking guns they had trained on Thack's chest.

The scene terrified Nicole. Opening her eyes, she stared at the rocky hills and raked her mind to think of a way to help Thack. Common sense told her that there was not enough time to get back to the ranch, collect some of Thack's men, then return. But she had to do something.

A low murmur broke her concentration. Drawing a deep, calming breath, Nicole turned carefully to take another peek into the shack. She saw Thack's lips move and heard the even tenor of his voice. She could hear only one word clearly. That word froze her blood.

Cocaine. Nicole's mind spun, her breathing became constricted, her pulse raced. Jason and cocaine. Pain. Death. Drugs. Fear closed in on her. The sunlight dimmed. She felt faint. But she couldn't faint. Thack needed help!

Parting her lips, Nicole gulped air into her trembling body. The scent of heat and dusty earth filled her senses. The world righted itself completely with the sound of unpleasant laughter.

"Too bad, Ranger, but you do understand that we can't possibly allow you to leave here alive." The man's voice was smooth, well modulated and all the more frightening because of its even tone. "We're not discussing a few hundred dollars here. We're talking about millions."

They were going to kill him! They were going to shoot Thack! Nicole's mind screamed the warning. She *had* to do something! All thought ceased, and Nicole went rigid as a hand was clamped over her mouth. Against her lips she could feel the roughness that was not skin and smell the distinctive odor of worn leather. Her breath eased from her as a barely discernible whisper filtered into her ear.

"Don't make a sound, love. Don't even move."

J.B.! A sob of relief swelled Nicole's throat, and she shut her eyes against a rush of stinging tears. J.B.! *Oh, thank God!* Nicole's eyes sprang open again at the sensation of his lips moving against her ear.

"I need your help." Nicole nodded. "Okay. Listen carefully, my love. I'm unarmed, but I'm going in there." Nicole stiffened and started to shake her head. The gloved hand held her still. "I must. Thack will die if I don't. Now listen. I want you to create a diversion. Hold out your hand, palm up." Nicole obeyed. Her cupped hand was filled with pebbly dirt and large stones. J.B. whispered to her again. "When I leave, I want you to start counting slowly to twenty. Then I want you to move clear of the window and hurl those stones as hard as you can at those vehicles over there. Okay?" Nicole drew a deep breath and nodded. "Start counting." J.B. removed his hand from her face. Crouching, he scooted beneath the window and around the corner of the cabin.

Nicole began counting immediately. On the count of twenty, she sucked in her breath, stepped around the side of the building and threw the handful of stones at the two vehicles. There was a rattle as the stones struck the metal. Nicole heard a startled cry from inside. Instinctively she stepped forward to glance into the cabin.

Still in a crouch, J.B. burst into the room at a run. Catching Thack at the hip with one shoulder, J.B. knocked him to the side out of the line of fire, just as a gun was discharged. The bullet missed the tall rancher by mere inches. And then Nicole witnessed the street cop in action.

With all the power and litheness of a ballet dancer, J.B. leaped into the air. Angling his body, he kicked out with one foot. The heel of his boot struck one man's hand, sending the gun he was holding arcing into the air. At exactly the same moment J.B. slashed out with his right arm, landing a vicious chop on the other man's wrist, knocking the weapon he was gripping to the floor. In an instant Thack was all over the first man, and J.B. was dealing with the second. It was finished in minutes.

"What's taking them so long?" Swinging away from the window, Nicole crossed the living room to drop into a chair.

Seated in the opposite chair, Barbara smiled serenely. "I've always felt that police work was ninety percent red tape. J.B. and Thack will be back as soon as they've waded through the formalities in San Antonio."

"How can you be so calm?" Nicole jumped up to stride back to the window. "Thack could have lost his life out there!"

"But he didn't," Barbara said, sighing with relief, "thanks to you and J.B." Her lips tilted into an impish grin. "Thack is definitely a man, and a man's got to do—"

"What a man's got to do," Nicole finished the adage in a dry tone, raising her eyes in supplication.

"Trite, maybe," Barbara murmured. "But true nonetheless."

A man's got to do what a man's got to do. Mulling over her friend's words, Nicole stared sightlessly at the ranch yard. She'd never felt so scared in her life as she had while out at that line shack. But then, Nicole reminded herself, she'd never before felt so much admiration for a man as she had while watching J.B. in action out there. Oh, yes, Josh Barnet certainly lived up to his nickname, tough hombre. Would she have him be any other way?

Shaking her head sharply, decisively, Nicole strode toward the door. "I'm going over to J.B.'s place." She glanced at Barbara. "Will you tell him?"

Barbara smiled and nodded. "I'll tell him."

The sun trekked west. The shadows grew long. Nicole waited. Impatience abrading her nerves, she prowled around the small house, wincing as her glance fell on a hanging plant. Agitated, she had watered all the plants at least three times, probably drowning the poor things. She had made fresh coffee—twice. She had dusted the tables and straightened the chair cushions. She had vacuumed the house. She was slowly going crazy.

And then she heard it. Nicole's head snapped up, and a sob escaped her throat at the sound of the truck coming to a screeching stop outside. Running to the door, she pulled it open as J.B. came up the walk in a loping stride. He stopped less than three feet from her.

"Hi."

Nicole didn't answer him. She didn't even think. She didn't need to think. With a strangled cry she launched herself into his arms. Lifting her off her feet, J.B. carried her into the house.

"I love you. I love you. I'll always love you." Arching into J.B.'s thrusting body, Nicole repeated the vow between gasps of exquisite pleasure. "With my heart and my body and my mind, I love you."

"You'd better," J.B. growled, skimming his lips over the scar from her shoulder to her cheek and then to her mouth. "Because I'll never let you leave me now."

His mouth claimed hers as forcefully as his body had claimed her moments before. Rational thought surrendered to sensations. Low murmurs had no substance yet held all the meaning in their world. Breathing grew ragged, strained, then, for an instant, ceased entirely.

"Josh! Oh, Josh!" Nicole's cry rang sweetly in J.B.'s ears, then his body bowed and stiffened.

"I love you, Nicole. God! How I love you!"

Nicole fell asleep with the sound of heaven singing in her head.

"I'm going back to work." J.B. glanced up from the coffee cup cradled in his hands and gazed across the table at Nicole.

The long day was over. Darkness shrouded the land. The rustle and twitter of night creatures drifted through the kitchen window. Staring into the softened eyes of the man she loved, Nicole straightened her shoulders and smiled.

"I understand—now. You belong back on the street."

J.B. blinked, then laughed. "Do you know what you just said?"

Nicole nodded. "I've seen the street cop in action, remember?" Her smile was soft. "I was off base up at the lake. I was wrong to accuse you of using your work as an ego builder. You *are* your work." The gold in her eyes flashed with annoyance. "And I think it's long past time your superiors realized it!"

"Hey, lady, calm down." J.B. grinned. "You sound like an irate woman defending her child—or her lover." His grin slipped, his hands tightened around the cup. "Or her husband," he added in a low, uncertain tone.

Nicole went absolutely still for a moment, then she held out her hand to him. "Is ... was ... that a proposal?" Her throat was dry, her heart was pounding, her breath was a memory.

J.B. carefully set the cup on the table, then grasped her outstretched hand. His voice went even lower. "Yes."

Nicole's breath came back with a whoosh. Her fingers laced with his. Her eyes brightened with a sheen of tears. "I accept," she said simply.

For a moment J.B. looked undecided. Then he nodded. "There was a woman, before the accident," he said abruptly. "We were engaged." His eyes darkened with remembered pain. "She had been after me to quit the force long before the accident. This—" he inclined his head to indicate his arm "—was the deciding factor."

"I know. Barbara told me." Nicole's lips tightened. "She was not only a coward, she was also a fool."

"You can live with less than—" he hesitated "—a whole man?"

"Joshua." Nicole's tone held warning.

"And you really won't object if I go back on the street?"

"I'll worry myself sick," she admitted. "But no, I won't object."

J.B. looked at her steadily, his eyes bright with pride and love. "I've accepted the office and the desk."

Stunned, Nicole gaped at him. J.B.'s face was free of doubt. He had found his own personal resolution. Sheer joy exploded inside her, radiating through her eyes and her smile. Yet she needed to be certain he had made his decision for the right reasons. "Are you positive this is what you want, Josh?" she asked intently. "Are you absolutely positive?"

His eyes were clear, steady. "Yes." He smiled wryly. "Something Thack said to me a couple of days ago set me to thinking."

"What did Thack say?"

"That my talent lay in investigative work." He shook his head. "The more I thought about it, the more I realized that he was right on target, as usual." His smile was breathtaking. Slowly he drew her hand to his mouth, reverently kissing each finger before going on. "And you were right, too." He bit her knuckle delicately when she would have protested. "Yes, you were. I really believed I needed to be on the street, but I don't.'' His beautiful voice was as much of a caress as his adoring lips. "I'll be doing work I love, and that's what's important.''

Nicole blinked against a rush of warm tears. "Yes, love, that's what's important.''

"Now the question is, can you accept living in Fort Worth?'' His eyes were watchful and uncertain.

Reaching across the table, Nicole slid her other palm over the black-gloved hand. "I can work for a brokerage firm anywhere.'' Her lips curved into a slow, sensuous smile. "I will joyously live in Fort Worth as long as I can live there with my own tough hombre.''

* * * * *

Get reacquainted with characters featured in Joan Hohl's trilogy for Desire in FALCON'S FLIGHT—Leslie Fairfield and Flint Falcon's story. Don't miss it—available in November from Desire!

Silhouette Desire

**Available
August 1987**

ONE TOUGH HOMBRE

Visit with characters introduced
in the acclaimed Desire trilogy
by Joan Hohl!

The *Hombre* is back!
J. B. Barnet—first introduced in *Texas Gold*—
has returned and make no mistake,
J.B. *is* one tough hombre . . . but
Nicole Vanzant finds the gentle,
tender side of the former
Texas Ranger.

Don't miss *One Tough Hombre*—
J.B. and Nicole's story.
And coming soon from Desire is
Falcon's Flight—the story of Flint Falcon
and Leslie Fairfield.

D372–1R

☿ Silhouette Desire
COMING
NEXT MONTH

#373 INTRUSIVE MAN—Lass Small
How could Hannah Calhoun continue to run her boardinghouse with any semblance of sanity when all her paying guests were pushing her into the all-too-willing arms of Officer Maxwell Simmons?

#374 HEART'S DELIGHT—Ashley Summers
Cabe McLain was resigned to a life of single parenthood—but that was before Laura Richards showed him that her childhood friendship had ripened into a woman's love.

#375 A GIFT OF LOVE—Sherryl Woods
Meg Blake had learned early on that most problems were best dealt with alone. Matt Flanagan was the one to show her otherwise—teaching her firsthand the power of love.

#376 SOMETHING IN COMMON—Leslie Davis Guccione
Confirmed bachelor Kevin Branigan, the "cranberry baron" from STILL WATERS (Desire #353), met Erin O'Connor—and more than met his match!

#377 MEET ME AT MIDNIGHT—Christine Flynn
Security agent Matt Killian did things by-the-book. He had no intention of having an unpredictable—and all too attractive—Eden Michaels on his team. But soon Matt found himself throwing caution to the winds.

#378 THE PRIMROSE PATH—Joyce Thies
It took an outrageous scheme from their respective grandparents to find the adventurous hearts beneath banker Clay Chancelor's and CPA Carla Valentine's staid exteriors. Neither imagined that the prize at the end of the chase was love.

AVAILABLE NOW:

**He could torment her days with doubts
and her nights with desires that fired her soul.**

VITA VENDRESHA

He was everything she ever wanted. But they were opponents in
a labor dispute, each fighting to win. Would she risk her brilliant
career for the promise of love?

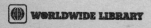 **WORLDWIDE LIBRARY**